# AFTERNOON MEN

# BOOKS BY ANTHONY POWELL

### NOVELS

*Afternoon Men*
*Venusberg*
*From a View to a Death*
*Agents and Patients*
*What's Become of Waring*
*O, How the Wheel Becomes It!*

### A DANCE TO THE MUSIC OF TIME

*A Question of Upbringing*
*A Buyer's Market*
*The Acceptance World*
*At Lady Molly's*
*Casanova's Chinese Restaurant*
*The Kindly Ones*
*The Valley of Bones*
*The Soldier's Art*
*The Military Philosophers*
*Books Do Furnish a Room*
*Temporary Kings*
*Hearing Secret Harmonies*

### BIOGRAPHY

*John Aubrey and His Friends*

### PLAYS

*The Garden God* and *The Rest I'll Whistle*

### MEMOIRS

*To Keep the Ball Rolling*
Vol. I. *Infants of the Spring*
Vol. II. *Messengers of Day*
Vol. III. *Faces in My Time*
Vol. IV. *The Strangers All Are Gone*

# Afternoon Men

\*   \*   \*

## ANTHONY POWELL

LOS ANGELES
SUN & MOON PRESS
1997

Sun & Moon Press
A Program of The Contemporary Arts Educational Project, Inc.
a nonprofit corporation
6026 Wilshire Boulevard, Los Angeles, California 90036

First Sun & Moon Press edition 1997
10 9 8 7 6 5 4 3 2 1

This book was made possible, in part, through contributions to
The Contemporary Arts Educational Project, Inc.,
a nonprofit corporation.

Cover: Charles Demuth, *Vaudeville: "Many Brave Hearts Are
Asleep in the Deep,"* 1916
Design: Katie Messborn
Typography: Guy Bennett

LIBRARY OF CONGRESS CATALOGING IN PUBLICATION DATA
Powell, Anthony [1905]
*Afternoon Men*
p. cm — (Sun & Moon Classics: 108)
ISBN: 1-55713-284-4
I. Title. II. Series.
811'.54—dc20

Printed in the United States of America on acid-free paper.

# CONTENTS

"…as if they had heard that enchanted horn of Astolpho, that English duke in Ariosto, which never sounded but all his auditors were mad, and for fear ready to make away with themselves…they are a company of giddy-heads, afternoon men…"

*The Anatomy of Melancholy*

# PART I—MONTAGE

"When do you take it?" said Atwater.

Pringle said: "You're supposed to take it after every meal, but I only take it after breakfast and dinner. I find that enough."

They stayed downstairs where the bar was. Upstairs there was a band, but dancing had not begun to any extent yet because it was still early in the evening. The room downstairs was low with a bar running all along one side of it and some tables and a few divans. The windows in the wall opposite the bar were all open, but they looked out on to a well, so that the room was really quite stuffy and there was a smell of ammonia. Several people they knew were sitting at tables or up at the bar, but they found a place to themselves in the corner of the room and sat down. Pringle said:

"If you pay for this round and give me three-and-nine-pence we shall be all square."

Atwater, thinking about the brandy they had drunk at dinner, did not say anything. The quality of the brandy had been poor. But he gave Pringle half a crown, a shilling and three pennies. They sat there without speaking, until the waiter had finished taking the order of a large party at the other end of the room and came over to them. Pringle said:

"I shall stick to brandy."

"Doubles?" said the waiter.

"Doubles," said Atwater.

Pringle said: "As far as I am concerned, I should like never to see a woman again. I should like to retire to the country and paint. In fact, I'm negotiating about a house in the country at the moment."

Atwater did not answer. He read a newspaper that someone had left on the table. He read the comic strip and later the column headed "Titled Woman in Motor Tragedy." He was a weedy-looking young man with straw-colored hair and rather long legs, who had failed twice for the Foreign Office. He sometimes wore tortoiseshell-rimmed spectacles to correct a slight squint, and through influence he had recently got a job in a museum. His father was a retired civil servant who lived in Essex, where he and his wife kept a chicken farm.

"How long has this place been open?" said Pringle.

"Not long. Everybody comes here."

"Do they?"

"Mostly."

They had met in Paris three years before, when Pringle had been trying to get a significance into his drawings of the short poses at Colarossi's, and Atwater was with a family at Saint-Cloud, where it was supposed he would eventually learn to speak French. It had been one night at the Coupole Bar. From the first they had felt a certain mutual antipathy, but, by contrast and comparison, fellow countrymen had seemed more nearly tolerable that evening than might actually be the case in other surroundings. But for some reason the acquaintance had persisted, and quite often they went out together when Pringle was in London, long after the earlier reason for putting up with each other's vagaries had been forgotten. Pringle came of a go-ahead family. His father, a business man from Ulster, had bought a Cézanne in 1911. That had been the beginning. Then he had divorced his wife. Later he developed religious mania and jumped off a suspension bridge. But, although he had ill-treated his children during the religious period, he left them all some money, and Pringle, though he did not much care for parting with it, had a comfortable income. His early life had made him painfully inhibited and he was a naturally bad painter, but a dreadful veneer of slickness picked up in Paris made people buy his work occasionally. Pringle was twenty-eight, and his red hair, for which he had been well bullied when younger, gave him more than a look of the traditional Judas. He sat there wearing a French workman's blue shirt and patent leather shoes. At times he twitched nervously and fidgeted with the things on the table.

"The trouble about women," he said, "is that you can't trust them." It was only a fortnight since Olga had left for good and, although it was an immense saving, the thought was still an irritating one.

"Say when, sir," said the waiter.

"When," said Pringle. "If I went to the country now and did some painting I could probably get another small show in the spring."

Atwater offered him his cigarette case but did not look up from the story of the accident. It was a knight's wife in a Bentley and on the Brighton road.

"What do you think?"

Brooding over dinner's cognac, Atwater said:

"I should do that."

"Have you heard anything of Undershaft?" said Pringle, changing the subject because he had in effect nothing to add to the plans for the projected reorganization of his life, and Atwater, having heard these at dinner, was evidently unprepared to take an active part at that moment in their precise rediscussion.

"He's in New York."

"Playing the piano?"

"Playing the piano."

Atwater put down the paper and looked round the room. He saw that Harriet Twining was sitting at the bar beside a man with a fat back to his neck. She was in a coat and skirt and looked very fair and dazzling. She had fair hair and a darkish skin, so that men often went quite crazy when they saw her, and offered to marry her almost at once. But when it came to the point she never married anyone, because either she got tired of the man after she had been about with him for a time or else the man said he could not stand the pace, or that he simply had no more money to spend. She waved to Atwater, who knew her slightly, and came over to where they were sitting. Without looking at Pringle she said:

"Are you coming to the party tonight?"

Atwater said: "I can't. I'm a dying man. Whose party is it?"

"You must come."

"I haven't been asked."

"Come with us. We'll take you."

"Who are we?"

"Me and my fat friend."

"Who is he, Harriet?"

"He's called Scheigan."

"Is he?"

"He's an American publisher."

"Why is he here?"

"He's going to do my book when it's finished."

"Are you taking him to the party?"

"Yes, he's keen on parties. He says all the Irish are like that. Mad for enjoyment."

She went back to her stool at the bar. Atwater watched her. She walked with her shoulders slightly hunched and swayed a little for effect but not very much. The man with the fat back to his neck sat at the bar as if he were going to begin to climb over it at any moment, using his stool to take off from. He was smoking a cigar. Atwater said:

"Don't you know her?"

"They all look alike to me," said Pringle. "Has Undershaft written to you at all?"

"He's living with an Annamite woman."

"In New York?"

"He says she's pretty good."

"I can't say I like your club much," said Pringle. "What with the heat and one thing and another."

"It is hot."

"And then the people."

"Well, they're the usual people. You can't expect them to look different just because the club hasn't been open long."

"I don't like the place."

"Take me somewhere else, then."

"No," said Pringle. "We'll have one more drink here."

"Let's go somewhere else."

"No. Hector has just come in."

"I insist on you taking me somewhere else," said Atwater. But Hector Barlow came across the room towards them. He was with another man.

"How are you both?" he said. He was a painter, stockily built with light eyes and hair that grew long down on his forehead in a widow's peak of black stubble. He was sucking a pipe and wore thick sack-colored clothes. Atwater had met him in Paris with Pringle, who had been at the Slade with Barlow. Atwater said:

"Come and sit with us."

"You don't mind my brother, do you?" said Barlow. "He's in the navy. He's on leave and goes back tomorrow."

"Yes, I go back tomorrow," said the brother. He was quite like Barlow, only cleaner and better-looking and he had brushed his hair, which was fair instead of being black. He was in a blue suit cut rather like a uniform.

"What will you drink?" said Atwater. "Waiter, bring a membership form. Mr Pringle is going to join the club."

"No, no," said Pringle. "Nothing of the sort."

"You must. I can't pay for you all the evening."

"Yes, you'd better join, Raymond," said Barlow. In social and intellectual matters Pringle showed a tortured deference to his opinions, although he always said that he considered Barlow an undisciplined painter. Pringle had the best of it in the end, because he used to lend Barlow money and ask for it back at awkward times, but Barlow in periods of affluence publicly contradicted everything that Pringle said and forced him to do things he disliked. His greatest triumph had been to make Pringle buy an expensive saloon car, but while he had been away in Paris one Christmas Pringle had sold it and resumed the use of the debased vehicle to which he was accustomed, and on his return waning finances had undermined Barlow's influence. Pringle saw him through the bad period following, but it was a great thorn in Barlow's side that Pringle had never bought one of his pictures. This was a card that all Barlow's assertiveness had never forced him to play. Barlow sat down on the chair next to Atwater. Atwater said:

"What's your life been like?"

"Hard," said Barlow, "hard. I had to get up early this morning."

"To paint the ambassadress?"

"Absolutely."

"Why should I join this club?" said Pringle.

Atwater said: "It will be cheaper for you in the long run." He said to Barlow's brother: "You get your gin cheap in the navy, don't you?"

"I'm taking him to some sort of party tonight," said Barlow. "Are you going? It's his last night on shore and all that."

"No."

"Why should I become a member?" said Pringle.

"You'd much better," said Barlow. "We all want you to."

"I suppose I shall be forced to. William has had a letter from Undershaft. He's in New York, living with an Annamite and playing the piano."

"Is he making any money?"

"Doing very well, he says."

Harriet Twining came over from the bar again. She said: "I have to have an occasional rest from my friend."

"Bring him over," said Atwater.

"Who's the new beauty?" she said, only just loud enough for the others to hear.

"Hector's brother. He's in the navy."

"A sailor?"

"Something of the sort."

"Bring him to the party."

Atwater said: "I'm not coming to the party. I'm going home to die."

"Give me a shilling," she said.

"I haven't got a shilling."

"You must have."

Atwater found a shilling for her. She put it in a gambling machine by the bar, pulled the lever hard, and banged the glass front. It spun a row of fruit and some money fell into the slot. She took it out and put it into her bag. Atwater said:

"Give me my shilling."

She gave him one of the coins.

"This is a franc."

"Oh hell," she said, "I suppose they'll all turn out to be francs."

She found a shilling for him and went back to her seat at the bar. The man with a fat back to his neck slipped his arm through hers. Barlow's brother said:

"That was a jolly pretty girl you were talking to."

"I'll introduce you to her later on."

"Oh, I say, will you?"

"Don't lend her any money."

"You mustn't debauch my brother," said Barlow. "He's got to go back to sea tomorrow. His leave is up."

"What's her name?" said the brother.

"Harriet Twining."

"She's a dangerous woman," said Barlow. "You'd much better steer clear of her."

His brother laughed uneasily and sweated at the back of his neck. The room was getting crowded and too hot. People came and looked about for somewhere to sit and then went away again. Some of those who could not get seats did not go away but stood talking or gaping at each other. The ammonia smell was persistent but ciga-rette smoke made it less noticeable as time went on. Walter Brisket came in. He was looking a little petulant. He had an inquiring small face and he stood with one hand on his hips and said:

"Hullo, William.

"Hullo."

"Shall I see you at the party tonight?"

"Who's the blond?"

"Hector's brother. He's in the navy."

"My dear, is he?"

"He says so."

"Is he coming to the party tonight?"

"We can't prevent him."

"I hear Undershaft is in Boston, living with a woman of color."

"He's in New York. I had a letter from him."

"I shall be so acid when I see him."

"Why?"

"He and his women."

Pringle said: "The smell in this club is awful."

"It is bad."

"It always smells like this," said Barlow. "I asked the secretary about it once. He said it was done deliberately. I don't remember why."

Pringle said: "Now I have become a member I shall write and complain of the club smell."

"You get your drink cheap in the navy, don't you?" said Brisket to Barlow's brother. Pringle leant across towards Barlow.

"How's Sophy?" he said.

"Not so bad."

"Are you taking her to the party tonight?"

Barlow looked at Pringle sluggishly, estimating whether he was being drawn or whether Pringle was merely being tactless.

"She doesn't enjoy parties," he said.

His brother said: "I say, how do those gambling machines work?

"I'll show you," said Brisket. "But isn't it time to go to the party yet?" He pulled back the sleeve of the brother's coat, so that he could see his wristwatch. Harriet Twining came over from the bar. She said:

"It will soon be time to go to the party. May we come and sit with you? You must meet my American friend. His Christian name is Marquis. Isn't it sweet?"

She smiled fascinatingly at Barlow's brother.

"Bring your fat man over," said Barlow. "He can sit on my knee. Or Raymond can give him his seat and sit on the floor."

Harriet beckoned to the man with a fat back to his neck, who began to climb down from his stool and come towards them.

"This is Mr Scheigan," she said.

She introduced them. They found a chair for Mr Scheigan somehow. He was bald but seemed to be bearing up well. He was carrying a bottle of gin, out of which someone had already drunk a lot, and he put his feet down very heavily when he walked. He said:

"I'm pleased to meet you, Mr Atwater. I hope you will excuse this bottle. It's pure habit."

"Forget about it. We'll get some clean glasses in a minute or two."

Mr Scheigan sat down suddenly and they put a chair underneath him just in time. He must have been about fifty and he was breathing a bit heavily. He had a blue chin. He said:

"We're all humans here anyway."

Harriet said: "Is it true that Undershaft is in America, living with a High Yaller?"

Brisket said: "That's one thing. The other is that Susan Nunnery has left Gilbert."

"She's so lovely."

"Very special."

"She's sweet," said Harriet. "I adore her. Don't you think she's sweet, William?"

Atwater said: "I've never met her."

"You must have seen her."

"No, I've never seen her."

"You must have."

"I haven't."

"I say," said Barlow's brother. "Do any of you ever go to the Forty-Three?"

"Aw," said Mr Scheigan. "Don't gossip. Let's enjoy ourselves. Let's have a good time."

"Tell him about your museum," said Harriet. "He likes culture. We might be going to the party soon."

Atwater said: "How do you like England, Mr Scheigan?"

Mr Scheigan said: "Hell, I haven't thrown a regular party since I've been over. But I've got a little apartment in St James's and all you folks must come and drink a bottle of wine with me there one of these days."

Pringle, who had been examining Harriet at close range and had only heard the last few words, said:

"Is it a bottle party?"

"You'd better bring a bottle of something," said Barlow, "in case there isn't anything to drink at all."

"Will that fair girl be at the party?" said his brother to Atwater in a whisper. Barlow said:

"I should bring a bottle of gin if I were you. You could get it here."

"Half a bottle should be plenty," said Pringle. "Though I don't see why I should bring anything at all as I haven't been asked to the party."

Mr Scheigan said: "You British never enjoy yourselves. I want to meet a few regular boys. I want to have a good time."

"There will be some at the party," said Atwater. "You ache with enjoyment there. I quite wish I were coming."

"I think it's time to start," said Harriet.

"No. We shall be much too early."

"Let's have one more round here before we go. It's safer. There may be nothing to drink there at all."

Mr Scheigan poured out the last few drops of his bottle into Harriet's glass. He then dropped the bottle on the floor. It made a lot of noise, but it did not break and rolled under a table a little way off, where it remained, as no one took the trouble to fetch it, although Mr Scheigan repeatedly asked that someone should do so and even threatened to get up himself. Mr Scheigan leant across the table towards Harriet. He said:

"I'll say you're pretty sweet."

"Mind," she said. "Don't upset the table."

Mr Scheigan took her arm again. The atmosphere was beginning to tell on him. He said:

"Baby, you're only a little kid, that's what you are."

"Be quiet."

"Baby…"

Atwater returned to reading the paper he had found in the earlier part of the evening, but for politeness sake he held it folded up under the table. The heat in that room was very oppressive. Barlow said:

"When is your show, Raymond?"

"Thursday week."

"Don't forget to send me a card," said Brisket. "I can't afford to miss a private view."

"Why, there you go," said Mr Scheigan. "Talking business. Why can't we all have some fun? I want to throw a party somewhere. Harriet here wants to throw a party. Mr Atwater wants to throw a party. We all want to throw a party. And yet we go on sitting in this goddamned hole talking business. I want to meet the bunch."

"You shall," said Barlow. "You shall meet the bunch, Mr Scheigan. You deserve to, after all the time we have spent in this club."

In the general movement to rise from the table, Mr Scheigan upset two glasses, which broke, but he could walk without difficulty. The waiter said:

"There's a bill of yours from the night before last, Mr Barlow. Would you like to settle it now?"

"Not particularly."

"The secretary said he'd be much obliged if you could do something about it."

"The only suggestion I can make is that I should write you out a cheque. But it would be waste of both our times."

"They're always bothering you in this club," said Brisket. "Never a moment's peace."

"I don't think they should be encouraged. Tell the secretary I'll settle it when I next come in."

The waiter shook his head gloomily and went away.

"Come on, boys," said Scheigan. "I want to throw a party."

Barlow said: "Yes. We're going to meet the bunch. Come on."

"Had you a hat?" said Harriet.

"Me?" said Mr Scheigan. "A hat?"

"Find his hat, someone."

"This one, miss," said the porter.

"Put it on his head," said Harriet. "I must repair my face."

They went into the street, where it was still hot, but coming out of the club the air seemed fresher. Two Shakespearian murderers, minor thugs from one of the doubtfully ascribed plays, were loitering outside and whistled up between them a pair of taxis. Atwater said:

"I still think I should be wiser not to come."

They waited for Harriet. Barlow's brother said:

"I say, will it be all right our not being changed?"

Harriet came out.

"Here's the address," she said, "on the back of this envelope."

She and Mr Scheigan got into one of the taxis and the rest of them into the other. Pringle became involved in an altercation with Second Murderer as to whether or not the latter had earned an emolument and, if so, whether three-pence was an adequate one. Pringle also paid for the taxi when they arrived, but was able to recover enough from the others to be well in hand over the combined transactions.

The party had begun by the time they arrived and was a good one, except that the flat that it was being given in was not big enough to hold all the people who had decided to come to the party. It was a nice flat with very up-to-date electric light fittings, but at the same time it was not big enough and it was already beginning to be in rather a mess. Some of the guests were in fancy dress and several were in evening dress. A few of those who were in evening dress stood about and looked surprised, and the host himself, a red-faced man wearing a white tie, was evidently not used to parties. But his wife, who was really giving the party, kept on telling him to talk to someone or to fetch drinks, so that he had no time to interfere or complain when people did things that he did not like. His wife was tall and rather splendid in a way, but she was not thin enough, and she had a nose that spoiled her appearance. She was very well dressed. Barlow's brother said:

"Is it all right our coming in?"

Barlow introduced him to all the people who were standing near.

"This is my brother," he said. "He's in the navy. He has to go back tomorrow."

When he had done this he sat down beside Atwater on a sofa in the far corner of the room and said:

"Raymond thinks I should marry Sophy. I admit he's a bad painter. But he knows both of us well. Or is it jealousy? Does he suggest it to ruin my career?"

"Is it urgent?"

"If I marry Sophy," said Barlow, "I shall never see anybody but my own friends. If I marry Julia, I shall never see anybody but her friends. A third course would be Miriam, who anyway might refuse to marry me when it came to the point. It would also mean living in the country."

"In comfort?"

"At least in luxury."

"You must make up your mind one way or the other."

"They are fine people, the Jews," said Barlow. "What I like about them is they always act on clearly defined principles. You know where you are with them."

"She's a nice girl, Miriam."

"Yes. I shall marry her," said Barlow. "I shall marry her and become a Jewish painter. There are no structural objections."

"It's a good life."

"I shall do that."

"You're very wise."

There were a lot of people dancing in the middle of the room and there was a gramophone and noise and a smell of make-up. Harriet had lost interest in Barlow's brother, who for the time being had found some people to amuse himself with in the other room. Harriet herself was dancing with Mr Scheigan. Someone stopped the gramophone, and Brisket, who had been sitting in front of the piano for some minutes, began to play in a burst of syncopation of varying loudness. Barlow got up from the sofa to dance with someone or other. Pringle, who was standing near fidgeting with his drink, sat down in the place beside Atwater and said:

"Poor Hector."

"Why poor Hector?"

"To my certain knowledge he proposed to three women last week. All comparative strangers. And was accepted by all of them."

"Really ?"

"Of course, one knows that sort of thing doesn't really matter, but the ties he's already formed make things so difficult."

"He forms ties, certainly."

Pringle said: "It wouldn't be so bad if his work was more promising."

There was not much space on the sofa. The room was now very crowded and the couple dancing trod on their feet. Atwater had a headache and wondered why he had come. He saw Barlow's brother moving through the door, laughing a great deal. He seemed to have made a lot of friends. Atwater said:

"What has happened to Mr Scheigan?"

"He's in the next room. With his girl. What did you say her name was?"

"Harriet Twining."

"I think I shall go and ask her to dance with me."

"I should."

"Do you think she will?"

"I don't know."

"What do you think?" said Pringle. He was shy of women, but tenacious, so that in the end they sometimes put up with him and even liked him. He always got rid of them when they began to like him. It did not happen often but it was a circumstance that was very distasteful to him. He could not deal with them when they were like that. In fact he hated them. Olga had not been like that. She had put him through the hoop. Atwater said:

"It's a question I can't attempt to answer. The worst she can do is to refuse."

It was at that moment of time, when Pringle was speculating as to the probability of his comparative success or the reverse with Harriet, that a glass of beer was upset over his legs. It was quite full and was lightly dropped into his lap by a girl who was standing beside the sofa. Someone had collided with her and had knocked it out of her hands. The beer splashed over Pringle's legs and on to the floor.

"Sorry," said the girl.

Pringle wiped the beer from his knees with a handkerchief, already rather grubby. He twitched horribly and his face went red in patches in curious contrast to his hair. The girl said:

"I'm so sorry."

Her expression was oafish, but it was on the whole this quality that gave her face a certain retentive efficacy. She had the look of a gnome or prematurely vicious child. But underneath the suggestion of peculiar knowingness an apparent and immense credulity lurked. Her rather rabbit-like appearance hinted at salient teeth but somehow she had escaped these, although their protrusion would not have altered materially the set of her face.

"Are you sitting on my bag?" she said.

"No," said Pringle, "I'm not."

He got up, his trousers clinging to him, and very angry. He did not say anything. Twitching, he just looked angry. He went through the crowd of dancers with a furious face. The girl sat on the sofa next to Atwater. She said:

"Is your friend angry?"

"Yes."

"I was looking for my bag."

"Were you?"

"It was suddenly knocked out of my hand and all over him."

"He's very wet."

"I expect he'll be able to dry himself somehow."

"There must be some way."

"Will you get me another drink," she said.

"What?"

"Anything."

It was becoming difficult to reach the table with the bottles and glasses on it. When Atwater arrived at it there were no clean glasses, so he took one that had a red drink in it and washed it out with soda water. Then he went back across the room. It took some minutes to get anywhere near the sofa. Waiting to pass people, he watched the girl on the sofa. She was wearing rather unlikely clothes and he thought he had seen her before somewhere. She might have been an art student, perhaps, brought along unexpectedly. Her general tendency was to resemble an early John drawing, but she had adapted this style to the exigencies of the fashion of the moment. The ensemble was not strikingly apt. He gave her the drink.

"I'm called Lola."

"No, really?"

"Yes."

"Who calls you Lola?"

"I just call myself Lola."

"Weren't you christened that?"

"No."

"One must have a name?"

"What's your name?"

"William," said Atwater. "I was christened it. I'm still called that."

"William is quite a nice name."

The heat was getting worse again. Brisket had left off playing and sat in front of the piano looking at the music. His drink was on the keyboard and he was smoking. Atwater saw the man who was the host and who had a red face come up to Brisket and heard him say:

"The gramophone is out of order, so my wife says will you go on playing."

"Nobody seems to want to listen," said Brisket. "They all talk."

"She says it's the least you can do."

Brisket, getting pettish, said: "I know I wasn't asked. But I can't play all the time."

"I know. It's her message and not mine."

"Will people listen if I go on playing?"

"I'll do my best to make them."

"I mean, I don't play just for my own pleasure."

"Nor mine," said the host. "I hate music. Even Gilbert and Sullivan. It's my wife."

Brisket began to play again, very loud and fast. Lola said:

"I don't know all these people. Wauchop brought me."

"Did he?"

"Yes."

"Are you a friend of his?"

"I go to his classes."

"Are you a painter?"

"I do posters."

"What sort of posters?"

"Will you come and see them?"

"Of course."

The party continued to be crowded. Mr Scheigan danced past them with Harriet. "You're just my little baby," he was saying, "that's what you are." Atwater saw Barlow's brother elbowing his way through the crowd, waiting for the music to stop so that he could get hold of Harriet. He always arrived just after Brisket had begun to play again and Harriet and Scheigan had once more begun to dance. His movements were beginning to be without decision. Lola said:

"Do you read Bertrand Russell?"

"Why?"

"When I feel hopeless," she said, "I read Bertrand Russell."

"My dear."

"You know, when he talks about mental adventure. Then I feel reinspired."

"Reinspired to what?"

"Just reinspired."

"Do you feel hopeless now?"

"Rather hopeless."

"Do you really?"

"A bit."

"Come back with me to my flat," said Atwater, "and have a drink there."

"Why?"

"We might talk."

"What about?"

"Well, inspiration and so on."

"Can't we talk here?"

"It's very noisy, isn't it?"

"I suppose it is."

Atwater said: "I've got some rather interesting first editions. I should like to show them to you."

"No. I must go home. I'm tired."

"So am I tired," said Atwater. "That's no reason why we shouldn't talk quietly at my flat."

"I don't think I will."

"Aren't you interested in books?"

"Awfully."

"Do."

"No," she said. "Really I can't."

The red-faced host had been pushed by the crowd behind the sofa on which they were sitting. He was standing in a cramped position against the wall. A squat woman in naval uniform made her way across the room and took his arm. She said:

"You're host, aren't you? Two girls have fainted in the bathroom and can't get out."

"Nonsense. I don't believe it."

"They can't."

"There's no lock on the door," he said. "I took it off before the party started."

## 3

The gramophone was working again now. The party was a little less crowded, but people seemed to be tired of dancing. Someone had fallen down in the corner of the room. Atwater could not see whether or not it was Mr Scheigan, but thought it looked like the cut of his suit. Harriet had disappeared. Barlow's brother was wandering about, finishing up several drinks that had been abandoned by their owners. Pringle had returned to the sofa. His trousers were still wet and he was wearing a false nose that gave his face an unaccustomed dignity. Lola sat very close to Atwater on the sofa. Pringle said:

"I've just seen your friend Harriet go off in Gosling's car."

"Have you?"

"Yes."

Atwater, who had fallen into a coma, watched the door opposite him. He was tired of the party, but had not the independent volition to leave it. The doorway was clear for a moment and as he watched it a girl who was coming through stopped on the threshold and, before she passed into the room, paused and looked round at everyone. She was not tall and she had big eyes that made her seem as if she were all at once amused and surprised and at the same time disappointed. It was as if it had been just what she had expected and yet it had come as a shock to her when she saw what human beings were really like. Also she had not the appearance of belonging to the room at all. She was separate. Her entrance into the room made her the immediate object of perception. It was the effect of a portrait painted against an imaginary background, an imaginary landscape even, where the values are those of two different pictures and the figure seems to have been superimposed. Atwater watched her. Barlow said:

"She's a bit of a menace." He was eating a sandwich and looking at the girl in the doorway.

"Who is she?"

"Who is who?" said Pringle, adjusting his false nose, which had given him a new lodestone for spasmodic movements of the hand. Barlow said: "Susan Nunnery."

Atwater said: "That's Susan Nunnery, is it?"

"That," said Pringle, "is Susan Nunnery. You know, these trousers of mine are ruined. I shall never be able to wear them again."

Lola clung to Atwater's arm.

"I'm tired of this place," she said.

Atwater said: "We'll go in a minute." He watched Susan Nunnery walking across the room and saw a man talk to her for a moment. Then they began to dance. The squat woman reappeared. She had spilled food down the front of her uniform. She said:

"One of the girls *has* fainted. But they've got her out."

The host, who was still behind the sofa and leaning against the wall, said:

"Has she, and have they? And who are *they,* may I ask?"

"Well, Naomi Race and Wauchop and Naomi Race's taxi driver and the policeman who was having a drink downstairs."

The host said: "If she's fainted, why get her out? The bath is the safest place for her. Left about here, she'll get trodden on by some of this riff-raff. Was she asked to the party?"

The squat woman said: "They both were, her friend says. And now they're sorry they came to the sordid, horrible party."

"I'll go and see about it," said the host, as he went away, beginning himself to look tired of the party. Barlow said to Pringle:

"Why are you wearing that nose?"

"Naomi Race gave it to me."

"I should stick to it."

"I say, how do you mean? Wear it always?"

"Every day."

"Don't be absurd."

Barlow said: "Yes, yes, I mean it. Has anyone seen my little brother anywhere?"

Atwater said: "Ought we to do anything about Scheigan? Now that Harriet has disappeared."

"He's quite happy on the floor. He needs sleep, I expect."

"He ought to be moved a bit," said Pringle. "People are tripping over his head. He's becoming a nuisance."

Barlow said: "Nonsense. I like seeing him there. He gives the room a lived-in feeling

"He lets down the tone of the party."

"Not so much as when he's awake."

"Oh, come."

"What do you think, Susan?" said Barlow. Susan Nunnery had left off dancing and was standing near them. She had a cigarette in her mouth, but it was not lighted. She said:

"About what?"

Barlow pointed to Scheigan. Lola said to Atwater:

"Shall we go now?"

"Yes. We'll go soon."

Susan Nunnery, looking at Scheigan, said:

"Isn't he a pet? He's so tired." She said: "Have you got a match?"

Barlow said: "I'll see if I can find some."

Susan Nunnery looked at Atwater. She said: "Give me a light off yours." She said: "No. I can reach it," as he moved his arm from behind Lola.

Pringle said: "You can't do that, Susan."

"I must for once."

Lola said: "Shall we go back now and have a drink at your place."

"We will."

The host appeared again. He was more red than ever in the face. He said:

"Come and dance with me, Susan. There must be some consolation for all this."

Barlow yawned. Brisket came over to him and said:

"Where is your brother?"

"In bed, if he's feeling half as tired as I am."

The room was getting empty. Susan Nunnery and the host were the only couple dancing. He circled round her heavily, his hand on her back, spread out like a pachydermatous growth or alien bunch of fruit. Beyond them on the left, Mr Scheigan began to get up from the floor. People treading on his face had roused him at last. He lifted himself on to his hands and knees and from there stood up. He stood rubbing his eyes for a little and then came across the room towards them. He said to Atwater:

"This is a bum party."

"Do you think so?"

"Yeah."

"It's nearly over, so you won't have to stay much longer."

Mr Scheigan said: "I never manage to throw a party in this cock-eyed country. Now, if you boys would come around to my place, we'd have a swell time."

As it happened, no one would go along to Mr Scheigan's place, but it was a long time before it was possible to make this clear to Mr Scheigan himself. Then they had to explain to him that Harriet had gone away without him. This he would not believe at all. He said:

"But she said she was coming right back to wish me good night."

Barlow said: "But life is like that, Mr Scheigan. You must have learnt that by this time."

But Mr Scheigan had not learned it and he was very, very angry. Barlow fetched him a drink, in the hope that it would cheer him up, but it only made him more unhappy. He sat down in an armchair and a tear ran down each of his cheeks. He said:

"My little cutie has gone and left her old man Scheigan."

He wept a bit and they gave him some soda water. Barlow said:

"If you have any left I should smoke one of those cigars of yours, Mr Scheigan. You will find it will cheer you up."

Mr Scheigan said that they were regular fellows and it was agreed that all present should meet at his flat at an early date. Atwater looked round the room and noticed that Susan Nunnery seemed to have disappeared. He heard Barlow say to Mr Scheigan:

"Take my advice in future and steer clear of women."

They all went downstairs and lent a hand in getting Mr Scheigan into his taxi. He got out once, but they put him back again, and as the taxi drove off they saw him leaning through the window talking to the driver. The taxi door came open as it turned the corner at the end of the street, but as long as the vehicle remained in sight Mr Scheigan had still not fallen out. Barlow said:

"He seemed quite unused to getting into taxis."

On the way back up the stairs they passed Susan Nunnery, who was coming down. She was with two men whom Atwater did not know. As she passed, Atwater said:

"Good night."

"Good night," she said. It was rather dark and she did not look at him. Then she suddenly turned round and stopped for a moment. She had her head rather on one side and looked at him. She said:

"Oh, good night."

She and the men with her went on down the stairs. Barlow said to Pringle:

"Why were you fumbling in Scheigan's pocket? Did you get anything valuable?"

"I was only putting in one of my cards."

"Your visiting cards?"

"One of the cards for my private view."

Barlow said: "What a very good idea. I expect he'll buy the whole lot. He took a deep breath: "I wish I'd given him my address," he said. And then he added: "That was a good idea of yours." He was impressed.

The room had become fairly empty when they came back to it. Lola was still sitting on the sofa. Atwater had forgotten about her and he was surprised to see her again so suddenly. He was filled with a feeling of intense irresponsibility towards all human creatures. That evening he did not wish to talk to anyone any more. He wanted to go home to bed. Lola said:

"Did you get your friend a taxi?"

"Yes, we got him a taxi."

"I expect we ought to be going soon ourselves."

"Perhaps we ought."

He tried to remember where they were going to go. Surely nowhere would be open at this hour? The red-faced host strolled across the room. His wife had disappeared and he said to them:

"I wish to goodness you people would go home to

bed. Have you any idea what the time is? Or do you expect to breakfast here?"

Barlow said: "Is there such a thing as a little more soda water and if I don't see you again, thank you so much for a really very enjoyable party." He said to Atwater: "Hasn't it been a good party."

"Wonderful."

Barlow said: "It's been a wonderful party. I wish Undershaft had been over here for it."

"Yes."

"Don't you think he'd have enjoyed it?"

"I do."

"So do I," said Barlow. "I'm sure he would."

Lola said: "We're going back now, aren't we?"

"Come on," said Atwater. He was feeling sleepy, but he got up from the sofa and went into one of the bedrooms on the other side of the hall, where he had left his hat. In the bedroom a man was lying face foremost on the bed. Atwater examined him and found him to be Barlow's brother. Someone had trodden on Atwater's hat. He sat down on a chair and began to straighten it out. He felt sleepy and angry. Barlow's brother opened his eyes. He looked at Atwater.

"Steady the Buffs," he said.

Atwater went out into the hall. Barlow was standing there looking at some lithographs that hung on the walls. He said:

"I don't expect you've seen my naval brother anywhere, have you?"

Atwater said: "Yes. He's in that room resting"

43

## 4

When they were in the street they walked for a little way. It was cooler now. Someone had dropped a bottle on the pavement in front of the house, so that the glass crunched under Atwater's feet as he walked over it. A taxi crawled by and they got in it. Lola had become sleepy and dozed on his shoulder, and Atwater wondered if the last drink had knocked her out or if it was the air after the heat of the party. The streets were empty except for men in Buffalo Bill hats and top-boots with hoses playing jets of water along the road. The taxi roared as if it were going soon to break down. Lola woke up a little. She said:

"Do you live near here?"

"Yes."

"So do I."

"I work in a museum," said Atwater. He was getting sleepier and felt he ought to say something. He had begun to be depressed.

"That must be very interesting work, isn't it?"

"No."

"Isn't it really?"

"I often think of running away to sea."

"I think it must be very interesting."

"Do you?"

"Yes," she said. "I do."

He hoped she wasn't going to begin on Bertrand Russell again. The taxi stopped. They got out and climbed the stairs leading to his flat.

"Do you live here, then?"

"Yes."

"What a sweet room," she said. She had woken up completely now. She sat on the sofa. Atwater also sat on the sofa, but only because the chairs in his room were too uncomfortable to sit on. He felt sleepy and could not remember why he had asked this girl back to his flat. He looked at her and thought she was like a gnome.

"Will you have a drink?"

"What have you got?"

"There's some gin, I believe."

"What else?"

"There may be some soda."

"I'll have gin and soda."

Atwater poured her out some gin and soda in a tumbler.

"Fancy our not having met before," she said.

"Fancy."

"Do you know Gwen Pound?" she said.

"I've seen her."

"I live with her."

"I see."

They sat on the sofa.

"Do you like me?" she said.

"You're a pet."

"Fancy our not having met before."

Atwater wondered why he was not enjoying himself more. Lola showed signs of becoming sleepy again. She put her legs up on the sofa. "I love your flat," she said. "What does it consist of? She had excellent ankles. Atwater felt sleepy and disinterested.

"Have another drink?"

She had another drink and made a face.

"What about your books?"

Atwater stood up. He could not do all the stuff about the books. He was too sleepy. He said:

"There are these. And then there are those."

"Darling," she said.

"Darling," he said and patted her on the head and kissed her.

"Do you read a lot?" she said.

"Sometimes."

"So do I."

"Do you?"

She finished her glass and made a face again.

"Darling, I feel so sick."

Atwater said: "You can't be sick here. This is my sitting room."

"But perhaps I shall be."

"No, no. You mustn't."

"Anyway, I won't have another drink."

"Have a cigarette, then?"

"No, nor a cigarette."

"You'd better go to bed."

"Had I?"

"Yes, if you're not feeling well."

"Perhaps I had."

"Yes, I think you'd better."

Lola did not look well. She was pale and untidy and she had too much powder on the left side of her nose. And yet the oafish contour of her face still made her attractive in a way. She looked inquisitive, but in low health.

"Perhaps I'd better go back."

"I think so."

"I'll go back."

"Shall I ring up a taxi?"

"No."

Atwater said: "I shall have to go to bed soon myself or I shan't be fit for anything tomorrow."

"Then I'll go."

"We must meet again."

He went with her down the stairs. It was light outside and the houses were curiously gray, like the back cloth of a scene on the films. Everything seemed unreal and temporary. The air was still fresh, but it was going to be another hot day. There was one taxi on the rank at the end of the street.

"Shall I take you back?" said Atwater, insincerely.

"No," she said, "I'll walk."

"Good-bye."

"Good-bye."

They kissed. She walked a little way and turned and waved good-bye to him. Atwater waved. Then he turned towards the house and climbed the stairs again. He put the gin in the cupboard in the sitting room and

went into his bedroom and pulled the curtains. The sun
came through the curtains, but not enough to see properly, so he switched on the electric light. He cleaned his
teeth, undressed and got into bed. Birds in the garden
at the back of the house were singing, which prevented
him from going to sleep for some time.

## 5

Sitting in his room in the museum, Atwater read a book. The walls of the room were colored buff and olive-green. As he sat and read he thought about the party he had been to the night before. He read:

"...the isomorphic connection between the orifice of a glass and the hole of a guitar is the result of a unilateral comparison, since the relation exists between two objects, practically identical..."

He knew now that it had been a mistake to ask Lola back to his flat. It had meant that he had stayed up too late, so that this morning he felt no interest in practical criticism. Absolutely none. He was sitting thinking about this loss of interest when Nosworth came in. Nosworth said:

"Good morning, Atwater. You're looking pale."

"I had some lobster last night. I may have poisoned myself."

"I'm not feeling particularly well myself," said Nosworth. "Those shooting pains in my back have returned."

"Yes?"

"Yes," said Nosworth. He was approaching fifty, and very tall and yellow. He was a good archeologist, so they said, and he wore a hard, turned-down collar a size or more too large for him. His face stood out yellow against the buff distemper. He stood there without moving or speaking, with several heavy books under his arm, as if petrified, or like something out of the Chamber of Horrors. Atwater said:

"I need a revolving chair. Do you think you could mention it?"

"I'll do my best. It took nine years to get mine. However, I'll try. It is the overheating and the underheating of the rooms that makes work here so difficult in my view."

"It must tilt back."

"That kind all do," said Nosworth. He sat down beside Atwater's desk and began to make notes in a pocket diary. Atwater continued to read:

"...in fact it is only after having conceived his metaphor that he subjects it to preparations, mechanical if you like, which that surest plastic technician of the present day that he unquestionably is, subsequently studies, organizes, coordinates and exploits. No orismology, therefore, nor terminology, far less any stylization..."

Nosworth said: "I first began to feel those pains about five years ago. I was on a walking tour in the Lake District with a man from King's."

He did not look up. He wrote in his notebook. He wrote very quickly, as if to distract his thoughts from the malignities of his body. Atwater thought about the party and did not direct his mind towards the identification of Nosworth's symptoms. But he watched Nosworth writing. While he was doing this a boy came in with a card. He handed it to Atwater. It was grubby and on it was written: *Dr J. Crutch.*

"What does he want?"

The boy, an ill-conditioned youth, overgrown and with a cauliflower ear and freckles, stood farouchely clasping and unclasping his hands.

"What does he want?" said Atwater again and, seeing the boy had something in his mouth, looked away. After some thought the boy said:

"He wants to see you."

"Me personally?"

"Asked to see somebody."

"Has he a student's ticket?"

"M'm."

Atwater turned to Nosworth, who was still writing up his engagements.

"Would you care to see him?"

"No."

"Tell him that personal interviews are only given by appointment. If he insists, find out details."

The boy went away. Atwater hoped for the best. Nosworth said:

"On certain evenings I cannot get to sleep. Then I drop off at about two or three in the morning and wake up again about four. Then the pains begin. They start in the lower part of the spine and spread slowly up my back. Sometimes my left leg aches steadily."

"This morning I have spots before the eyes. However, I expect that will pass off."

"You don't look well," said Nosworth, and was about

to continue his own diagnosis when the boy came in again. He still had something in his mouth. Chewing gum, Atwater suspected. The boy said:

"Gentleman would like to see somebody about the exhibits in room 16."

The man was evidently a professional nuisance.

"The ones in case B?"

The boy nodded his head. Atwater felt rather angry. It seemed impossible ever to get any serious reading done, with Nosworth talking about his health and people bothering all the time. Nosworth looked up from his book and said:

"I warned the standing committee that we should have trouble about those subordinate figures used in the initiatory rites. Of course, my advice was not taken. They all said the room was too dark for anyone to notice them."

"I noticed them myself," said Atwater. "Especially the one on the left."

"One of these days," said Nosworth, "there will be a repetition of what happened in that room two years ago."

"Or worse."

"Still, I suppose you'd better see him."

Atwater said to the boy: "Ask him to wait. I'll see him as soon as I can. Give him a chair."

"It wants repairing."

"What does?"

"The waiting room chair."

The boy slouched off.

"Wait a moment," said Nosworth. "What happened to Miller this morning?"

"Varicose veins," said the boy. "All his family have them on and off."

He went away.

"There's no discipline in this building," said Nosworth. "Absolutely none. I'm not complaining, I'm merely stating a fact."

Atwater closed his book. It was one of the days when he was not in the mood for reading. Faces appeared and disappeared on the printed page. He said:

"The weather is very stuffy."

"It's a lot that," said Nosworth. "When the pains have spread over my back and my legs are aching, my mouth goes quite dry. When that happens I know I'm in for a bad time. It sometimes happens as often as twice a week."

"It's a hopeless position."

"But I shall be boring you. What are you doing tonight? We might dine together and go to a talkie. I want to see *She was a Yes Girl.*"

"I'm dining with Mrs Race."

Nosworth shook his head. He said:

"Dear me. Well, I hope it's a good dinner."

The boy came in again and handed Atwater a document folded in four and greasy. As a labor-saving device he stood a long way off and held it towards Atwater at arm's length. Atwater took it from the boy's hand, just within reach.

"What is this?"

"Gentleman told me to give it to you."

Atwater took the paper and unfolded it. It was a pamphlet and was called: "A short introduction to an expository treatise on, and a critical examination of, the former international agreements for the proposed unification of craniometric and cephalometric calculations: together with some directions and suggestions for collecting more exact information and suitable specimens for anthropometric measurements to be made on living subjects for physical anthropology: by J. Crutch, MRCS, etc."

Atwater handed the pamphlet to Nosworth, as it seemed a quicker method than reading it aloud. Nosworth glanced at it and said:

"Now I come to think about it I believe he came in about five years ago. But Huntly interviewed him. It was before Huntly died, you see."

"I suppose he's mad."

"Oh, yes. Quite, I imagine. But I don't expect he'll keep you long."

Atwater put down his book, marked the place with a piece of blotting paper and went into the outer room.

The visitor was standing there, smiling quietly to himself. He was about sixty and was wearing a mackintosh and a very silly hat. He had evidently bought the mackintosh when he was a young man and had always worn it a good deal. He had a white mustache and looked definitely dirty. Atwater said:

"Can I help you?"

"Help me?"

"Yes," said Atwater, "help you."

"Oh, yes. Of course."

As there was only one chair, too unsafe to sit on for any length of time, both of them stood up. Atwater said:

"You were saying?"

The old man with the white mustache, Dr Crutch in short, looked away and smiled as if a little embarrassed. He said:

"It was only an unimportant matter."

And then he talked in a low voice about his life and how useful he could be to the museum. Atwater wondered how long he was going on and whether he was a lunatic or some semi-serious nuisance and work creator. He did not listen. He knew that the best he could hope for was that he should avoid hearing it all more than once. He considered other things. He achieved the complete detachment of thought of one who listens to the words of a schoolmaster. He became lost in his own introspections. The old man, Dr Crutch, continued to talk until his outline became blurred. Before Atwater's eyes he seemed to turn into one after another of the people who had been at the party and then back again. At last he paused, quite breathless, panting.

"You see," he said, "I have plenty of qualifications."

"Unfortunately qualifications are not enough."

"Not enough?"

"Insufficient."

"You don't think I shall be of any use to you?"

"Not actually of use. Of course, if you cared to leave your address..."

"You haven't anything in the way of indoor research?"

"Not, I fear, at the moment."

"And then," said Dr Crutch, "those cases in room 16, I wanted to speak to you about them."

"Yes."

"You see, I'm writing a book on the subject. You know what subject I mean, of course?"

"Of course."

"It is one that has to be very carefully handled to avoid giving any offense."

"I suppose so.

"I think I could do it."

"There is the standard work."

"It would supplement the standard work."

Atwater swayed slightly, an apparent vision of trelliswork before his eyes. His mouth was curiously dry. Again he wondered how long it was going on. In his ears the noises of the party hammered. The old man pursued his own train of thought and said:

"I don't expect you have read any of my books?"

"As it happens, I have not. I find I get very little time for reading."

"I'm not surprised. Though I expect you write yourself."

The situation did not seem to be developing. Atwater said:

"I do. But I have little time for that either. You see, I'm always busy."

Dr Crutch said: "We're all of us a bit inspired," and,

catching sight of Atwater's face, added: "I hope I'm not wasting your time."

"It's not a question of my time. My time is always at your disposal. But the government. One's duty to the State. *Pro bono publico* and so on."

"Then you don't think you can help me?"

"If you could tell me exactly what you want."

"Well, if you could spare a moment, it's like this," said the doctor, but did not speak. He looked thoughtfully at Atwater's head.

"Like what?"

"I was going to suggest about those images in room 16 that I might be able to make use of them."

Through Atwater's mind passed a picture, or rather an interminable reel, a lugubrious procession of close-ups, of all the trouble he would have if the doctor were allowed to examine in his own hands the images. Atwater said:

"I'm afraid it's very difficult to get permission to see the exhibits away from their cases. It would be a long time before it came before the standing committee and even then they might refuse."

The doctor smiled again in an embarrassed way. He said:

"I was going to suggest that you might dispose of them to me."

This was decisive. Atwater made a powerful effort not to show the relief that he felt overwhelming him in spite of the humming and clattering in his ears and the images before his eyes of light and fire. But Dr Crutch

57

had declared himself. The man had shown himself to be a genuine lunatic and not a borderline case who could create work for everyone on the staff. He was a bedlamite. A natural. The end was in sight.

"I'm afraid we can't sell them. We never sell anything, you see."

"Don't you?"

"Never," said Atwater. He added after: "We're prevented by an Act of Parliament."

"Are you?" said Dr Crutch. "Are you indeed?"

"Yes."

"There are far too many laws on the statute book. It would be a good thing if they expunged a few of them."

"It would indeed."

"I must have those images. I must have them for my book. I must have them for my book. I could give a very good price."

"Impossible, I fear."

"Perhaps some arrangement could be made."

"I fear no arrangement could be made on the basis you suggest."

The moment had come to act. Atwater said:

"Unfortunately I have an appointment. I regret I can be of so little use."

He then left the room with all possible speed. The situation had perhaps been saved. He hoped that it would be five years again before Dr Crutch reappeared.

He returned to his desk. Nosworth had gone away to his own room. The morning had still to be got through and Atwater thought of the various things that it was

his duty to do. First of all there was the minute on to-
tems to be drawn up. That was not urgent. It could, in
fact, wait. It occurred to him to begin writing a novel,
but his brain was almost at a standstill and it would be
a mistake to make a false start. There were several letters to be dealt with. Unacceptable invitations, bills,
definite demands for money. These might have to remain unanswered for a day or two as he did not feel
well that morning. Then there was the possible distrac-
tion of writing a letter to Undershaft in New York. That
sort of thing cleared the mind. It crystallized ideas. The
expression of gossip on paper put matters in their proper
perspective. Besides he wanted to hear more of the
Annamite. Or he might write to his own sister, who was
unhappily married to a man in the Indian Cavalry. But
he did not feel much like that either. Instead he sat and
thought about existence and its difficulties.

Later the telephone bell rang. Atwater felt shaken.
The secret of life had seemed at that moment not far
away. A few more minutes and absolute reality might
have been grasped. Now things were as far off as ever
before. Years of thought, years of labor, years of dissi-
pation might never bring the conception so near again.
He took up the receiver.

"...speaking...I'm sorry I can't hear...who?...
who?...*who*?..."

The voice at the other end of the line became more
faint. Atwater felt himself losing interest. The whirling
noises in his head had begun once more. He listened.
Whose name could be the extraordinary dissyllable that

the woman (or was it a man?) at the other end was trying to say. And then suddenly it came to him. The name
was Lola.

"...yes...of course, I should love to...yes...yes...no,
of course not...Tuesday, then..."

He hung up the receiver. There was the world making itself felt again. Once more material things forced
themselves forward. He made a note on his pad to go
and see her on Tuesday. What was he going to do about
her, he wondered, and thought of the gloomy intellectual affair he had had with his dentist's wife soon after
he had come to live in London.

Returning to more immediate questions, there was
the projected translation of the Finnish professor's
screed. That was urgent, being due on the following
Friday. Something might have to be done about arrang-
ing for that. An even more important matter was also
outstanding. The correspondence about the new geyser in his flat had to be readjusted. This fell into several
divisions: viz, letters to and from the landlord; letters
to and from the gas people; and, owing to a separate
involution, letters to and from the plumber. These main
sections were further complicated by the death of the
original plumber, a sickly old man, which necessitated
the employment of a new firm of plumbers, who had
bought up the goodwill of the business and, closely following on this eventuality, a change in the administra-
tive area of the gas people, which combined to delay
the matter and to increase the extent of the dossier.
Atwater felt that a rearrangement of this correspon-

dence and a sharp letter to his landlord, a retired haberdasher living at Berkhamsted, would clear his brain. While he was occupied in composing the opening lines of this letter the boy came in again and handed him a card. It was dirty, and on it was written: *Dr J. Crutch.*

The lout produced it with the air of a conjurer who is performing a well-known and rather irksome trick which he wants to finish quickly before progressing to something of more general interest.

"Again?"

"He wants his book."

"His book?"

"The book he gave you."

"Did he give me a book?"

"Folded up. I brought it," said the lad, with a great mental effort and moving the food diagonally across his mouth so that it lumped out the lower part of his cheek in a semicircle.

"The brochure," said Atwater. "God! the brochure."

The brochure had disappeared. On Atwater's desk lay the reports of the Old World Customs Society, 1906–08 and 1911–13. There were also some letters; several second-hand book catalogues; some time tables; wine lists; press cuttings; photographs of Minoan costume; boxes of envelopes; bits of blotting paper; and a few labels. The wastepaper basket was also full. Atwater searched. He searched the floor, the wastepaper basket and his pocket. Even the boy glanced about in mute assistance. The brochure was gone. Atwater went into Nosworth's room. Nosworth was writing.

"Have you got the brochure?"

"What brochure?"

"On the unification of craniometric and cephalometric calculations."

Nosworth continued to write. He was translating Danish poems for money. He said:

"My dear Atwater, what in the world are you talking about?"

"The paper the lunatic left."

"The lunatic?"

"The one who came this morning."

"Sir Gregory Williams?"

"No, no, no. The one you said came five years ago."

"Was it some story I was telling you?"

"Dr Crutch."

"Oh, yes," said Nosworth. He was not interested.

"You know what it means if we don't find it?"

"What?"

"He will come back here every day from now onwards until he is sent to an asylum, which may not be for years."

"You can deal with him."

Nosworth wrote steadily. He said:

"I want an attribute of the sea. *Wine-dark* for example. But that will hardly do. Can you think of anything?"

Atwater slung his bolt.

"My leave is quite soon," he said.

Nosworth paused and looked up. He said:

"Why should I have the brochure?"

They searched the room. The boy, who had strayed in behind Atwater, also glanced about furtively. The brochure could not be found.

"Your pockets?" said Atwater.

Nosworth turned out his pockets. They contained a number of unsuspected objects but the brochure was not among them. Then Nosworth looked through his note case. The brochure was there, folded between two ten-shilling notes.

"How more than odd," said Nosworth, and went on translating. Atwater gave the brochure to the boy.

"Run, or the gentleman will have gone."

Atwater walked slowly back towards his desk. It was being a difficult morning. But he took a pen and began to write a long complaining letter to his landlord, on the subject of the geyser. He was filled with a sense of unrest. In the middle of the first paragraph he was interrupted by someone standing at his elbow. It was the boy. The boy made a curious sound with his lips, tongue and teeth, a special whining scrape, produced by the sharp influx of air and intended at once to attract Atwater's attention and at the same time to indicate that there was no longer any considerable quantity of food in his mouth.

"Well?"

"Gentleman left word to say he couldn't wait. He'll be back tomorrow or the next day."

"Damn!"

The boy went away. Nosworth came into the room. He said:

"What day of the week is it?"

"Saturday."

"Oh, is it?"

"I think so."

The morning passed slowly. Atwater tore up the letter to his landlord. He went over to the window and, opening it, leaned out and watched the people below. Unexpectedly there was a faint breath of air that made the trees sway slightly. Hindu students in light gray flannel trousers were pattering across the grass. Their voices were carried up to the window:

"That's all right, old boy, though it's awfully decent of you."

Atwater, thinking of friendship, remembered that he was having tea with Barlow that afternoon. He went back to his desk and took up his book again and began to read:

"...instinctively drawn to the constant renewal of the data of his imagination, he is careful not to take certain products of the use of those data as the basis for new works. The form which he lends to a particular metaphor, or to certain specific relations of closely or distantly connected volumes, is never given to the elements of a picture *a priori,* but purely and simply in consequence of the developments required by the composition of a picture..."

## 6

Barlow had two rooms and a kitchen. There was a bed in one of them and all his clothes, which lay about on the floor. The other room was bigger. Barlow used it for a studio and it had a Victorian settee in the middle and a box mattress in the corner against one wall and canvases in and out of frames against the other walls. Sophy opened the door. She did not live there but Barlow had given her a latchkey. When she saw Atwater she said:

"Hullo, William."

"Hullo, Sophy."

"Barlow hasn't come in yet."

She smiled. She was fair and plump, a painter's girl, rather like an Eve by Tintoretto. She had some sort of a job in a dress shop. They went into the studio. Atwater took off his hat and sat down on the settee. Sophy, bulging out of her dress, stood with her hands on her hips looking at him. She always stood in good positions, better than a trained model, with her weight thrown in unlikely places.

"Has Hector done any more portraits of you?"

"You haven't seen this one, William," she said. She called all Barlow's friends by their Christian names but not Barlow himself. He was too important. She pulled a canvas out of the pile beside the fireplace. It was a nude of herself, sitting on a kitchen chair with a piece of chintz as a background. She said:

"It's nice, isn't it?"

"Put it in the frame."

She slipped it into one of the frames standing against the wall and lifted it on to the easel. She took a few steps back and with unseeing eyes looked at it with Atwater, smiling to herself a little as if she was too surprised really to believe the phenomenon of paint and canvas.

"I'll make the tea. Barlow will be in soon."

She went out, leaving the door open behind her, and he heard her rattling about plates, as she was clumsy in her moves.

"Did you like the party?" she said from the kitchen. Although Barlow did not take her to parties, she always showed a subdued interest in them.

"It was all right."

"Barlow was very queer after it."

"Was he?"

Atwater looked round the room, empty but at the same time full of things. Not unlike a box room, everything in it seemed provisional and as if it had been put in its present position only for a few minutes and left there because nobody would take the trouble to put it somewhere else. Barlow's pictures were good, but there were too many of them about. There were some books. Not many. One of them, Atwater noticed, was *Thus Spake Zarathustra*. Sophy brought the tea in and she was pouring it out when Barlow arrived.

"Sorry to be late," he said. "I've just been sick in a mews."

He kissed Sophy and said:

"Is tea ready?"

Sophy said: "I've just made it. William has only been here a minute."

Barlow said: "I've just been round to see Pringle. He showed me all his work for the last five years."

Sophy said: "He rang up this morning and asked me to tea in his studio today."

"The hell he did. At the shop?"

"Yes."

"How did he know the number? Did you tell him the name of the shop?"

"You were talking about it the other night. I expect he looked up the number in the book."

"What did you say?"

"I said I couldn't go because I was having tea with you."

"What did he say?"

"He said he'd ring up again."

"I shouldn't go if I were you," said Barlow. "He's a bloody man. You won't like him."

"I don't care for him specially."

"He's awful."

Sophy took up the teapot again and began to pour out the tea. Barlow turned to Atwater and threw up his eyes.

"Have some cake," he said. "It's rather stale."

Atwater said: "Do you know Susan Nunnery well?"

"What has she been doing?"

"Somebody was talking about her last night."

"Oh yes. She was there last night, wasn't she?"

"Yes."

"Is she still living with Gilbert?"

"Was she?"

"I don't know," said Barlow. "Perhaps she wasn't. I can't keep up with girls like that."

Atwater drank his tea. Sophy went out to get some more hot water. Barlow said:

"Miriam was here yesterday. I think really I'd better marry her."

"Why? Have you ruined her?"

"No."

"Why not?"

"I didn't think she'd like me to."

"She's a nice girl."

"Yes, I shall certainly marry her."

"Do you see much of her?"

"No, not much."

Sophy came in again. She said:

"The kettle is leaking. We shall have to get another one."

"I'll get one," said Barlow. He said to Atwater:

"Did I tell you I sold some things last week? Among them that small head of Sophy."

Sophy said: "The one that's like me."

"Yes. The one that's like you."

Atwater said: "What happened to your brother after I left last night?"

68

"He caught his train this morning."

"How was he?"

"He looked all right."

"I didn't think he looked all right at all," said Sophy. "Poor boy."

"His hand shook a bit at breakfast."

"He looked a treat," Sophy said. She nodded her head.

"He'll recover," said Barlow. "He'll be all right as soon as he gets back into the wardroom or the gunroom or the fo'c'sle, wherever people like him live when they're in their boat."

"It was a good party."

"Who did you go away with?"

"She's called Lola."

"Who is she?"

"She does posters."

"I thought as much," said Barlow. "You'll never get rid of her. You never get rid of girls dressed like that. What's she like?"

"She says she reads Bertrand Russell quite a bit."

"You'll never get rid of her. How did she come to the party?"

"Wauchop brought her."

"She's one of Wauchop's women, is she?"

"She goes to his classes."

"Wauchop produces women like that," said Barlow. "And then people like you and I have to spend all our spare time and money entertaining them."

"Yes."

"Are you seeing her again?"

"She rang up this morning."

"What did I say!"

"I'm rather fond of her."

"You're mad. However, we won't argue about little things like that. Are you coming to a cinema with Sophy and me tonight?"

"I'm dining with Naomi Race."

"Well, it's a meal," said Barlow. "It staves off the pangs of hunger. At least, it usually does. I remember on one occasion it didn't. It was during a period of trade depression too. I finished off the salted almonds."

Sophy lit Atwater's cigarette with a long spill. The downstair bell rang. Barlow said:

"Go and look through the curtains and see who it is, Sophy."

Sophy put down her tea and looked at the street from between the curtain and the side of the window. She peered for some time and then said:

"Fotheringham."

"Oh, it's Fotheringham, is it?"

"I think he saw me. He waved."

"He wasn't just staggering?"

"Are you sure?"

Sophy said: "Why, yes, of course." She laughed.

"Go and open the door," said Barlow. "Let him in if he's reasonably sober."

Atwater said: "I've met him with Undershaft once or twice."

"You must have met him thousands of times. I see him whenever I stir out of the house."

"I sat with him and Undershaft all one evening while he tried to persuade Undershaft to do an article on occult music for his paper."

Barlow said: "He's one of the sub-editors of a spiritualist paper. He says that of all classes he likes spiritualists least. It doesn't matter much, as he's only there to help make up the advertisement pages, and, as he himself says, the job is only temporary, so why grumble? He's only been doing it for five years."

"It must be a pleasant job on the whole."

"He wanted me to do a series of drawings of well-known spiritualists, but he seems to lose interest as the evening progresses."

They heard Fotheringham talking to Sophy all the way up the stairs. He came into the room in front of her, a heavily built young man with very pink cheeks. He had not shaved yet and he was carrying a bowler hat and an unrolled umbrella. The aura of journalism's lower slopes hung round him like a vapor. With a slight hesitancy of manner he said to Barlow:

"I say, dear old chap, I'm going to be frightfully rude. Do you mind if I use your telephone at once, Hector?"

"Over there on the packing case."

Fotheringham took up the receiver and gave a number. He smiled at Sophy.

"Frightfully rude of me. I do apologize, Sophy," he said, and then: "...Hullo, darling...yes, I know...I was so sorry...I was dreadfully sorry...really...really, I was...just a little...no, I'm afraid I can't...yes, of course...another time...good-bye, darling...good-bye." He hung up the receiver.

"Poor little thing," he said. "I hate disappointing her. But there it is. One has to be cruel to be kind sometimes, though I'm afraid it sounds a terribly pompous thing to say."

"Do you both know each other?" said Barlow.

Atwater said: "We've met with Undershaft. You've heard he's in America now?"

Fotheringham said: "And doing very well, I hear."

"Making some money."

"I expect I shall see him soon," said Fotheringham, "as I'm going there myself."

"When are you going?" said Sophy. Fotheringham rather fascinated her. He was the only man who ever took her attention away from Barlow even for a few minutes, and for some reason the only man whom Barlow never had his moments of regarding as a potential rival.

"The actual date isn't fixed yet. But it will be pretty soon."

"Are you giving up your present job?"

"It leads nowhere, you know."

"Why weren't you at the party?" said Barlow, who had begun to sharpen some pencils with one of the table knives.

"Party?" said Fotheringham. "Which party?"

"Last night's party."

"Oh, last night's party. I started off to it but somehow we never reached there. I got talking to a man I found in a little bar off the Strand, where no one much goes."

"Did it last all the evening?"

"He took me to a place he knew of called Ginger's Club. It wasn't very gay really."

Barlow put down the table knife. He said:

"Sophy, give the man some tea. Don't just sit gaping at him."

"No, no," said Fotheringham. "Not for me. I never touch the stuff."

"Anyway, what job do you expect to get?" said Barlow, picking up the knife again and speaking as if he would much rather not know what job Fotheringham was going to get. He would have liked to exercise over Fotheringham, as over Pringle, a domination, but a certain protean acuteness, well camouflaged, made Fotheringham immune from his influences. Fotheringham said:

"What I should really like would be something in the open air. Somewhere where you'd wake up in the early morning feeling really fresh and go out and do something strenuous and come back about eleven and have a pint of beer at the pub and then go on working until lunch and spend the rest of the day rubbing up the classics perhaps."

"The classics?"

"Oh Marlowe and all that lot, you know. Villon and so on."

Sophy said: "It's a pity we don't go down to the country sometimes."

Barlow said: "You know I'm always ill if I leave London for short periods."

"As it is," said Fotheringham, "I never seem to get any time for solid reading. Those spiritualists keep my nose to the grindstone, I can tell you, Hector. I often envy the leisure you painters have."

"All the vitality a painter has goes into trying to sell his pictures. And well you know it."

"Vitality," said Fotheringham. "That's the thing. One of the reasons I want to go to America is that I hear everybody there has such wonderful vitality."

Atwater said: "You must meet a friend of ours called Scheigan. He has a great deal of vitality."

"Will he get me a job?"

Barlow said: "If you can both meet at a sober moment he's bound to."

"You know, you may think me conceited, but I think I'm a bit too good for my present job."

"You can have a thirty-three-and-a-third percent commission on any pictures you sell for me. I can't say more than that."

"Now listen to me for a minute. I may not be as talented as you, Hector, or as beautiful as Sophy, but don't you agree that I'm wasted?"

"No. I don't think you are in the least."

Fotheringham laughed. He said: "Now you're joking. Be serious."

"Not a bit. You're very lucky to have a job at all."

"You don't mean it?"

"I mean what I say."

"No, that's absurd," said Fotheringham. "I don't believe you when you say things like that."

"It isn't absurd at all."

"Anyway, I must find a job. I should like to find something that brought me into touch with people who really mattered. Authors and so on."

Barlow sighed. He said:

"Sophy and I are going to the cinema at half-past six. We're going to eat after. Shall we go out and have a drink now?"

"But wait just a moment, Hector. Do you really mean that you think I'm not wasting my time on this paper?"

"Everybody is, in the building."

"You're merely offensive, Hector."

"I mean to be."

"You know, you go too far. People who don't know you as well as I do would never guess that you were joking."

Barlow took a peculiar small hat from beside the telephone.

"We are now going to have a drink," he said. He put the hat on his head.

"You're hopeless," said Fotheringham, and laughed.

"Come on."

They went down the stairs and out into the street. Barlow said:

"Where shall we go?"

Fotheringham said: "I know of a place."

"Is it far?"

"Just round the corner."

They walked down the street, Fotheringham swinging his unrolled umbrella and whistling a little through his teeth. They arrived at the place. There was no one else in the saloon bar, which was smart with heavy beaded curtains. The barmaid had a very elaborate permanent wave in her hair. She said to Fotheringham:

"And how are you feeling, young man?"

"Maisy, you know I owe you an apology for the other night."

"You go on."

"Now, Maisy."

"What are you going to say to me now?"

"Well," said Barlow, "what are we drinking?"

Fotheringham said: "No, these are on me."

The barmaid brought the drinks. She said to Fotheringham:

"You're a terror, you are."

"Now, Maisy, you mustn't say that."

"Don't go spilling your drink," she said.

"Maisy, was I really a nuisance?"

"No error."

Fotheringham said to Barlow: "It's awful. One has about two drinks and one becomes a nuisance."

"You're dangerously near being one of the people who are a nuisance before they've had two drinks."

"No more of that, please, Hector," said Fotheringham. He said to Atwater:

"Are you dining with anyone tonight?"

"With Naomi Race."

"Otherwise we might have had dinner together. However, give Naomi my love. I may look into her place later in the evening."

Barlow said: "Well, Sophy and I are going to our cinema. What about another round before we go?"

They had another round. Barlow and Sophy got up to go. Fotheringham said:

"Good-bye, dear old boy. Good-bye, Sophy, my love."

"Look in again some time," said Barlow.

"I will, I will."

They went out. Fotheringham said:

"What a nice girl Sophy is. I only wish I could find someone like that."

"There must be others."

"You're right. There are others. The question is, where to find them."

Atwater did not answer. He looked round the bar, which was full of looking-glasses embossed with red and blue and gold lettering. There was also a photograph of the Prince of Wales lighting a cigarette.

"Ah," said Fotheringham: *"Où sont-elles, Vierge souveraine? Mais où sont les neiges d'antan?"*

"Where, indeed?"

"I suppose that girl is in love with Hector."

"I suppose so."

"Not that I'd put myself in competition with Hector for a moment. But it's always interesting to know."

"Yes."

The barmaid, who was leaning on her elbows and looking at them, said:

"You haven't said you're sorry properly yet, Mr Fotheringham."

"You mustn't tease me, Maisy."

"Tease you, you say?"

"Yes, Maisy."

"Get along with you."

"No, Maisy, no."

The barmaid laughed. Then she took a swab and rubbed it over the counter, where she had poured too much peppermint into Atwater's gin and it had overflowed. She was not a pretty girl, but she had a sensitive face and very crinkly hair. When she had wiped the counter quite dry she went round to the other side of the bar where the cold snacks were and began to cut some ham sandwiches. Fotheringham sighed. He said:

"It is at times like this that I often think how little there is ahead of us, young men like you and I."

He turned his glass between his finger and thumb. He had become suddenly sad. Atwater said:

"The same again?"

"Please. What do we see before us? A vista of ill-ventilated public houses. An army of unspeakably tipsy journalists."

"Put them from your mind."

"A million barmaids all saying the same thing."

Atwater nodded.

"Drink that is so nasty one can hardly get it down. Women who are always tormenting."

"But America?"

"Ah," said Fotheringham, "America. But the date isn't actually fixed yet."

"Does that matter?"

"It may."

"Why?"

"You ask me why," said Fotheringham. "But I ask you, where is it all going to lead if I go there?" He had become very gloomy.

"Where is it all going to lead? I ask you that, Atwater."

"I don't know."

"No. You don't know. I don't know. None of us know. We just go on and on and on and on and on."

"We do."

"We sit here when we might be doing great things, you and I."

"Might we?"

"Do you know what we are doing?"

"No."

"Shall I tell you?"

"Yes."

"We are wasting our youth."

"Do you think so?"

Fotheringham said: "Every minute the precious seconds flit by. The hour strikes. Every moment we get a little nearer to our appointed doom."

"Which is?"

"Can you bear to hear it?"

"Yes."

"I cannot tell you. It is too horrible."

"I insist."

"For some, the corner seats in clubs under the meager covering of a sheet of newspaper. For others, the voices of little children, often and deafeningly shrill."

"We have the present."

"Tonight," said Fotheringham, "I am a man handicapped by his future. For me the present and the past do not exist."

"Try not to think about it."

"Now I'm beginning to realize what Hector meant when he said he did not think I was too good for my job."

"He never means anything."

"No," said Fotheringham. "No. Kind of you, sweet of you, to say that. But if Hector's words mean nothing to him they have come to mean a great deal to me. What a man. Talent. Genius would hardly be too strong a word. Beautiful women without number. The world at his feet. And what am I? What do I do? What can I say? You know, I often wonder that men like you and Hector will be seen about with me."

"My dear Fotheringham."

"I mean it."

"You can't."

"Yes, yes, I do."

"Don't say so."

Fotheringham picked up the two glasses. He said: "I shall say it and I shall repeat it."

"No, no. Don't repeat it."

"Yes," said Fotheringham, "I shall say it again, and more than once again, how fortunate I count myself to have such friends as I have; and whatever people may say about friendship, and no one knows better than I that it's a quality that in these days is often rated lower than those temporary emotional connections between this or that sex which have their foundations on soil as impermanent as the sand of the seashore, yet it is eventually a thing, in fact it is *the* thing, that in the long run the happiness of men like you and me, if you will forgive me for the moment in classing us both together, depends on most of all in this struggle, this mad, chaotic Armageddon, this frenzied, febrile striving which we, you and I, know life to be; and when we come at last to those gray, eerie and terrible waste lands of hopeless despair, unendurable depression and complete absence of humor that drink and debt and women and too much smoking and not taking enough exercise and all the thousand hopeless, useless, wearying and never to be sufficiently regretted pleasures of our almost worse than futile lives inevitably lead us to, when the vast and absolutely impenetrable mists of platitude or, in the case of some, of dogma envelop us and cover us up entirely, when we have given up the last feeble effort to keep up anything in the nature of appearances and have indeed sunk to those slimy horrible depths of degradation and misery and lowness that comes to those who would sell their name, their intellect, their mistress, their old school, their honor itself, for the price of a bitter; when love has come to mean the most boring form of lust, when power means the most useless pots of money, when fame means the vulgarest sort of publicity, when we feel ourselves exiled forever from the pleasant pastures of debonair insouciance (pardon the phrase), which is, I suppose, the one and really only possible mitigation and excuse for the unbridled incoherence of this existence of ours,

81

it is then, and only then, that we shall realize fully, that we shall realize in its entirety, that we shall in short come to know with any degree of accuracy— What was I saying? I seem have lost the thread."

"Friendship."

"That was it, of course. I'm sorry. That we shall realize what friendship means to each one of us and all of us, and how it was that, and that only, that made it all worth while."

"Made what worth while?"

Fotheringham made a comprehensive gesture with his hands.

"Everything," he said.

"As, for instance?"

"I'm not a religious chap. I don't know anything about that sort of thing. But there must be something beyond all this sex business."

"Yes."

"You think so?"

"Oh yes. Quite likely. Why not?"

"But what?"

"I can't help."

"You can't."

Atwater said: "But what has made you so depressed?"

"Depressed?"

"Yes, depressed."

Fotheringham finished his drink at a gulp. He said:

"I suppose I must have sounded rather depressed. You see, I had rather a heavy lunch."

"I see."

"You know how a heavy lunch always lets you down."

"About this time in the evening."

"Yes," said Fotheringham. "About this time in the evening. You know, I'm afraid I must have been boring you."

"Not a bit."

"I feel I have. You must forgive me. Do you forgive me? Say you forgive me, Atwater."

"I do."

"It's not the weather to eat and drink a lot in the middle of the day."

"Who were you lunching with?"

"I had lunch with George Nunnery. No doubt you know him?"

"Is he a relation of the girl called that?"

"Her father. You know her, then?"

"I've met her."

"She's attractive, don't you think? I can never make up my mind which is the best, her or Harriet Twining."

"They're both very good-looking."

"You must meet old Nunnery."

"I want to."

Fotheringham said: "He's one of those brilliant men whose mind has become a complete blank."

"Is he?"

"You can imagine what good company he is."

"Yes, indeed."

"All the brains and understanding there and never

the least danger that they are going to become a nuisance."

"Wonderful."

"As you say. Wonderful."

"When will you take me to see him?"

"Any time. Ring me up."

Atwater said: "I will. I shall have to go now."

"Why?"

"I have to dine with Naomi Race."

"You can't go yet."

"I must."

"No," said Fotheringham. "For goodness' sake don't go."

"I have to."

"You can't leave me like this."

"I wish I hadn't got to go."

"Have one more?"

"No."

"Yes, yes. You must."

"No, I can't."

"I insist, William," said Fotheringham. "For I shall call you William. I insist."

"No, no, I can't."

Suddenly resigned, Fotheringham said: "Ring me up, then." He said to the barmaid:

"Maisy, leave off cutting up all that ham and tell me exactly what I did the other night."

## 7

"I've had to make dinner a bit later," said Mrs Race. "I hadn't time to let you know."

She had not changed yet, but she was looking her best that night, and Atwater noticed that she had done her hair in a new way. No one knew how old she was or anything about the late Race except that he had known Rossetti and that Mrs Race had watched the first Jubilee with him soon after their marriage. She used to ask Atwater to dinner about once every two months. Atwater said:

"I saw you at the party last night. I wanted to talk to you but there was such a crowd."

"They're all coming tonight," she said. "Harriet Twining, Walter Brisket, Wauchop. Then there's a woman whose surname I can never remember. Her Christian name is Jennifer. You won't like her. I don't like her myself."

"Why have you asked her?"

"She does all my typing. It was her ambition to meet Wauchop. She admires him enormously."

"As a painter?"

"Yes. Especially the symbolical ones."

"Is that the whole party?"

"That's the whole party," said Mrs Race. "And now

I must go and change. You will find some books there and all the drink is in the cupboard."

She pulled her Chinese tea-gown round her and went upstairs. Atwater heard her calling to her maid. He went over to the bookshelf and, as there was a set of the Keynote Series level with his eyes, he took down *God's Failures* and sat in the armchair. He was still reading the story about the village idiot and the traveling circus when the woman called Jennifer arrived. She was about thirty-two and large-boned, dressed in a terra cotta colored garment and beads. Atwater poured out some sherry and gave her a cigarette. Mrs Race always had Russian cigarettes that tasted of strawberries and cream. They talked for a bit and Jennifer had just said that being in a museum must be very interesting work when Harriet and Brisket came in together. Harriet said:

"I found Walter in the street asking the policeman which house it was. Didn't I, dear? As if you haven't been here dozens of times."

"Here's Naomi," said Brisket. "You and your innuendoes."

Mrs Race, in a black dress and hung all over with châtelaines and little odds and ends, stopped for a moment to make a good entry through the door. Then she came in with a rush, saying:

"How are you, Harriet darling? And you, Walter?"

Brisket said: "What sequins, Naomi. You make me green."

"And Jennifer," said Mrs Race. "Do you all know each other? Of course you all do."

"Who are we waiting for, Naomi?" said Harriet.

Mrs Race said: "Wauchop! He's always late."

She poured out some more sherry. Jennifer said:

"No, no, really. I shall be so drunk."

Waiting for Wauchop, Brisket talked about where he was going for the summer and Harriet talked about the best way to smuggle scent. Mrs Race said:

"I've got a special Balkan liqueur that you must all try after dinner."

Harriet said: "Who was that oddity with red hair you were with last night, William?"

Atwater said: "He's called Raymond Pringle."

"Is he really?"

They heard Wauchop arrive and gather impetus by beginning to chuckle half-way up the stairs, so that he came into the room with the full force of a roar of laughter behind him. He kissed Mrs Race on the forehead and, taking hold of Harriet's hands in his, he swung them backwards and forwards, saying:

"Here we go gathering nuts in May, nuts in May, nuts in May."

Jennifer looked very excited. She knew that she was seeing life. Harriet said:

"You're getting fat, Wauchop. And what on earth has happened to your face?"

"Ah, ha," said Wauchop, "I thought you'd notice that. I've had it massaged this afternoon. I may grow a beard later in the year."

Jennifer said: "You know, I think more men ought to wear beards, though I suppose some men would look

87

rather funny in them and wouldn't be able to carry them off at all."

Atwater talked for a short time about beards in history. No one listened. Harriet said she did not like beards for men or women. Dinner was announced. They went downstairs to the dining room, which was at the back of the house and small, with one quite good Conder drawing in it, and a Staffordshire figure of St Peter on the mantelpiece. Wauchop sat on Mrs Race's right, next to Harriet, and Brisket on her left, next to Jennifer. Atwater sat at the end of the table. Wauchop said:

"And how are we all feeling after the party?"

He laughed a good deal.

"Not too good, I expect," he said. "Some of us."

He then told them what had happened to him at the party. Brisket interrupted him at regular intervals.

"How lovely Susan Nunnery looked," said Mrs Race. "Really I thought she was ravishing. She said she would come in and see me later on this evening."

Wauchop said: "She's a great little girl is Susan."

"She's quarreled with Gilbert," said Harriet. "And I don't blame her. That man ought to be shot. In fact, I may shoot him one day myself."

"Was she a friend of his?" said Atwater.

"My dear, when did you arrive?" said Harriet. "What was the country looking like? Is the grass as green as ever?"

"She seems very changeable," said Mrs Race.

"*Souvent femme varie,*" said Wauchop. "But I don't know what we should do without them."

Jennifer said: "Do you really think we are all like that, Mr Wauchop?"

Wauchop took too long to prepare his reply and his voice was lost in the noise of the telephone bell ringing. Mrs Race went to the side table, where the instrument was kept under a doll in a pink crinoline, and took up the receiver. She listened and said:

"It's for you, Harriet."

"So popular," said Brisket.

Mrs Race handed the telephone to Harriet, who sat down on the side of the table.

Jennifer said how much she admired Wauchop's pictures. Harriet said:

"...yes, darling...I'd love to...might be worse...I'll be there..."

She came back to the table. She said:

"I'm afraid I shall have to go rather soon after dinner, Naomi. You don't mind, do you?"

"Is it a party?" said Brisket.

Harriet said: "I shouldn't take you with me if it were, duck."

"I don't expect I should come, anyway," said Brisket. "Not without knowing more about it. I have my pride, though you might not think it."

Wauchop looked across the table at Brisket as if he did not like him much. Brisket stared back at Wauchop with his expression of eager inquiry. Mrs Race talked about all the books she had been reading. Dinner was uniformly nasty except for the Sauterne, which was good but tepid. Atwater said:

"I believe you know Nosworth in my museum, Naomi?" Jennifer said to Wauchop: "I was saying to Mr Atwater what interesting work I think his must be."

"But of course, a pet," said Mrs Race. "He used to have such nice ankles, though I don't know why I'm saying it, because I haven't seen him since before the war. How is he?"

"Rather diseased."

"Of course he's a man wholly without vice," said Mrs Race. "Though I must say I surprised him once skulking round Roedean when I was staying at Brighton years ago. He said he was on a walking tour."

"Don't you dote on girls' schools?" said Brisket, looking at Wauchop. Wauchop pretended not to hear. Harriet said:

"My dear Walter, don't be absurd."

Jennifer talked to Wauchop about his pictures. Harriet talked to Mrs Race about shoes.

Mrs Race said: "This is the liqueur. It comes from the Balkans. You must try it. Some people think it delicious. You'll have some, won't you, Wauchop?"

Atwater talked to Brisket about Pringle's last love affair.

"You know I never refuse a drink, Naomi," said Wauchop.

Harriet said she never drank any liqueur but brandy, and Brisket said his doctor had forbidden him to drink any liqueurs at all. The others had some.

"*Salute,*" said Mrs Race.

"Sweethearts and wives," said Wauchop.

Everybody drank. Atwater did not spit it out because he was used to drinking nasty drinks, and because he had only sipped it, and also he would have tried not to do so, even if he had taken more than a sip, out of consideration for Mrs Race's feelings. Wauchop drank his glass off at gulp and pushed his chair back and put his hand over his mouth. Atwater, from the end of the table, watched Wauchop's neck change color.

"Shall I pat you on the back?" said Brisket to Wauchop, but did not venture to do it. He and the others watched Wauchop's face and the veins swelling on his forehead."

"Don't you like it?" said Mrs Race. "Some people think it so good."

"It seems to me a little sweet," said Atwater, lighting another cigarette, and finishing the dregs of his coffee.

Jennifer had stood it very well. Like Atwater, she had only sipped it and she had just sat there red in the face.

"You'll be better soon, Wauchop," said Harriet. "You drank it too fast."

"Was it Susan Nunnery in a red dress at the party last night?" said Atwater.

Mrs Race said: "Don't you know her? She may be coming in tonight. Drink some water, Wauchop. You'll feel better then."

Harriet said: "Well, I must be off now, Naomi. Sorry to fly so early. See you again soon. I'll ring you up."

"Must you really, Harriet?"

"Must, darling, really," said Harriet. She kissed her hand and went out of the door. Mrs Race said to the company at large:

"She's sweetly pretty, isn't she? A touch of the tar-brush, of course, but that's such an advantage in these days. She could get anywhere if she took the trouble."

Brisket said: "Some of the best of us are quite unambitious."

"I should take your collar off," said Atwater to Wauchop. "I'm sure Naomi wouldn't mind."

"Yes, take your collar off, Wauchop," said Mrs Race. "If you're really feeling bad. I hate to hear you coughing in that way. We'll go upstairs and you can take it off there in the other room."

"I can give you a hand up the stairs," said Brisket, but Wauchop, still speechless, waved him away.

In the drawing room, Mrs Race turned on the gramophone. Unless prevented she would often play Wagner, but tonight she put on the records that she had bought during the war. They were nearly all of them noisy records and she preferred to use loud needles, so that the gramophone drowned Wauchop's coughing to some extent. Mrs Race said to Brisket:

"Will you look through this pile. My eyesight is bad tonight and I want to play you all *Belgium put the Kybosh on the Kaiser.*"

Jennifer said: "I love these old war tunes. Don't you, Mr Wauchop?" She had not tried to drink the rest of her liqueur and had soon recovered from the first sip. Mrs Race had insisted on Atwater bringing what was left of his upstairs, but he had taken the opportunity of her search for gramophone records to pour it into a vase of tulips. Wauchop did not answer, but he showed he was better by nodding his head. He sat there without his collar, with a very red neck.

"Where was Harriet going?" said Brisket.

Mrs Race said: "With Gosling, I suppose. That won't last long, unless she behaves herself."

"She was with an American called Scheigan last night."

"Was she?" said Mrs Race. "How are you feeling now, Wauchop?"

Wauchop said: "I got a frog in my throat." But the Balkan liqueur had subdued him a good deal. The records regressed chronically.

"This is one of the gems of the collection," said Mrs Race, putting on *Yip-I-Addy-I-Ay*.

Wauchop sat there grimly without a collar.

Brisket said: "Have you heard about Undershaft, Naomi?"

"The Siamese?"

"Yes."

Mrs Race said: "I think he's so wise."

The evening passed rather gloomily. Wauchop sat recovered, but collarless. Atwater and Brisket talked about Pringle. Jennifer looked through the albums of records. The bell rang downstairs. The maid came in.

"Miss Nunnery," she said.

Susan Nunnery came in rather quickly. She was in day clothes and a hat. She said:

"Hullo, Naomi. I didn't know you were having a party. I just looked in to say good night. I'm so tired I must go to bed at once."

Mrs Race said: "I don't think you know Jennifer. You know everyone else, don't you?"

"Yes, I know everyone else," she said. She looked at Atwater. Again he had the impression that she did not belong to the room and the background that she was in. She seemed separate, like someone in another dimension. He looked at her, but without any particular feelings except that he felt that she seemed separate. He wondered what it was about her that made him feel like that. Susan Nunnery said:

"Why aren't you wearing a collar, Wauchop?"

Brisket said: "Wauchop has just had a seizure. We thought we should have to dispose of the body."

Wauchop said: "Ah, Susan. We never seem to meet now."

He had recovered himself a good deal in the last few minutes and had almost got control of his cough.

"Why is it?" she said.

"If Wauchop had died," said Brisket, "we should have to have sewn him up in a sack and dropped him over the Embankment."

"Harriet has been here," said Mrs Race, "but she left very early."

"Harriet Twining?"

"She'll come to a bad end, if she doesn't take care."

"What has she been doing?"

"She has been behaving very injudiciously," said Mrs Race, who was evidently annoyed by Harriet's demeanor that evening.

Susan Nunnery said: "Well, I must go to bed. I really must. I haven't had any sleep for a month. I only came in to say good night."

"I'll take you back, Susan," said Wauchop. "I must be going too. Wait a moment while I put this collar on."

"Oh, are you going, Mr Wauchop?" said Jennifer.

"Don't bother," said Susan Nunnery. "You know it's out of your way."

Wauchop made a gesture to show how little trouble and what a pleasure it would be to him to go in a taxi with her. He had quite recovered. Susan Nunnery said:

"Well, good night, Naomi."

She turned half round.

"Good-bye," she said.

Wauchop went over to the mirror, an Empire piece with glass of the period, to see that his tie was straight. For some seconds he examined the gray distortions it made of his face. Jennifer said:

"Can I help you, Mr Wauchop?"

Atwater said to Susan Nunnery:

"When shall I see you again?"

"We might meet."

"Are you in the book?"

"Yes," she said, "I'm in the book. Under George Nunnery."

Brisket said: "You must take care of Wauchop this evening. He's not feeling well. I get my bus where you get your taxi, so I'll walk with you as far as there. In fact, on second thoughts, you will be able to give me a lift some of the way."

"Yes, of course we can," said Susan.

"Good-bye," said Mrs Race. "You must all come again soon."

Mrs Race, Atwater and Jennifer were left alone. Jennifer said:

"What a nice man Mr Wauchop is. What a nice man. And I know so well what great big men like that are like. They're always just big bundles of mischief."

"Wauchop's all right," said Mrs Race, "if he didn't talk so loud. I don't mind what he says as some people do. But he shouts it so."

"And fancy such a well-known painter being simple like that," said Jennifer. "No conceit about him. Great men are really like children, don't you think, Mr Atwater?"

"Yes."

"Of course all men are really like big boys. That's what I always tell my brother and he always says I'm quite wrong, and I expect you agree with him, don't you, Mr Atwater?"

"Yes."

"But you know you are."

"Are we?"

"Why, of course, you all are," said Jennifer. "Aren't they, Mrs Race?"

Mrs Race said: "You're looking sleepy, William."

## 8

"And how was Mrs Race?" said Nosworth.

Atwater said: "In good health."

"Who was there?"

"Wauchop among others."

"Was he? Well, well."

"You're very particular about whom you meet."

Nosworth said. "People who are particular about whom they meet are savages. Noble savages."

Outside it rained and rained and rained. The water poured down the gutters of the museum and a damp mark began to appear on the outside top corner of the wall in front of Atwater's desk. That day the museum was full of people who had come in to shelter from the wet, people who had never seen the inside of a museum before, who wandered about leaving puddles behind them, embarrassed by the exhibits and making self-conscious jokes to each other. Atwater, who had spent most of Sunday lying in bed, felt tired. He thought it over for some time and then rang up Susan Nunnery and asked her out to dinner. Lola telephoned later and changed the day that he was to come and see her.

# PART II—PERIHELION

# 9

When he went to see Lola, Gwen Pound, of whom Undershaft had once said that she looked the sort of boy who might win a scholarship in chemistry, opened the door. She and Atwater knew each other by sight. Atwater said:

"Is Lola in?"

"She's out at the moment."

"She'll be in soon, I suppose?"

"Was she expecting you?"

"Yes," said Atwater. "She rang me up."

"Did she?"

"Yes."

"Come in," said Gwen Pound. "She'll be in soon."

Atwater went in. The room had bits of stuff pinned up round the walls and two large red candles on the mantelpiece.

There was a divan, but nowhere else to speak of where you could sit. Gwen Pound said.

"Will you have a gasper? I'm afraid there's nothing to drink."

Atwater sat down. She said:

"You haven't been here before, have you?"

"No. Have you both lived here long?"

"Nearly two years."

She said: "I'm so sorry that we've got nothing here to give you to drink."

"I don't want a drink, really."

"We sometimes have drink here," she said. "But it seems to get drunk."

"Oh yes, I know."

"I always think it's so awful not to have a drink to offer people when they come in."

"No, really."

"Oh yes, I think it's awful."

She said: "Lola will be in soon, I expect."

Atwater said: "She should be in soon, because she told me to come in about this time."

"Did she ring you up?"

"Yes, she rang up."

Gwen Pound said: "You don't mind my going on making this, do you? I've got to wear it tonight."

Atwater said: "Of course not." He said: "What nice candles those are."

"Yes. They are nice, aren't they?"

"I rather like candles in a room."

"Yes, they're nice."

"Of course, the only time that I really use candles is when my lights fuse, which is quite often."

"We prefer them really. They throw such a nice light."

Lola came in soon after that. She had brought a bottle of sherry with her. She smiled at Atwater.

"Have you been here hours, William?" she said.

Gwen Pound said: "It's a very good thing you got

that. I've been saying that I was so sorry that there was nothing here to drink."

"Where's the corkscrew?" said Lola.

"Give it to me," said Gwen Pound. "I'll open it."

Atwater said: "Let me."

"No, I'll open it."

"Please let me open it," said Atwater.

Lola said: "Gwen will open it. She opens them very well."

Gwen screwed it well down into the cork and pulled. Nearly all of the cork came out at last and Gwen went out to fetch some glasses. Lola came across the room towards him. He took her hand. She said:

"Sorry to keep you waiting. How did you get on with Gwen?"

"All right."

"Did you?"

"Yes."

Gwen came back with the glasses. Her face was still rather pink from her efforts to get the cork out of the sherry bottle, which made her less uninviting. Lola said:

"Get something to strain it through, Gwen, so that it isn't all full of cork."

Gwen poured out through a handkerchief three glasses of sherry. She said:

"I'll have a quick drink before I go out."

Lola said: "Are you going out, Gwen?"

"Yes, I've got to go out."

"Where are you going?"

"Oh, I have somewhere I must go."

"Must you, really?"

"Yes, I have to, really."

"I'm so sorry," said Lola. "Otherwise we might all have dinner together."

"No, I have to go out."

"You haven't got to go away, have you?" said Lola to Atwater.

"No, I haven't got to go away."

"I must go very soon," said Gwen. "I thought I'd just stay and open that bottle for you."

"How sweet of you, dear," said Lola. "Wasn't that sweet of her?" she said to Atwater. Atwater said yes, he thought it was. Gwen cheered up a bit when Lola talked to her. She said:

"You know, I believe I can draw a cork as well as any man."

Lola said: "Of course you can, Gwen darling. I always said you could." She said to Atwater: "Gwen can draw a cork as well as any man, can't she?"

Atwater said: "Yes, of course she can. Why, some men can hardly draw them at all. At least, they always seem to go inside the bottle. I always seem to do that with them myself."

"Gwen hardly ever breaks them," said Lola. "Do you, Gwen?"

"No, I don't break them often certainly. This is the first one that I've broken for ages."

"Where are you going tonight, darling?"

"Oh, I don't expect it would interest you much."

"Where, darling?"

"With that dreadful old man."

"Oh, Gwen."

"He's a dreadful old creature. He's nearly seventy. You wouldn't believe the things he says," said Gwen, half to Atwater, who made a suitable face to express disapprobation and surprise.

"Gwen darling, is it wise?"

"I know how to look after myself, dear."

"Do you, darling?"

"Better than you do, my dear."

"I can't think why the old brute hangs round you so."

Gwen said: "Oh, he's not so bad really. He means well and he's very kind."

"But is he?"

"Oh yes, he means well."

"I'm not so sure of that."

"After all, dear, he's my friend and not yours."

"Oh, he's not at all my sort, Gwen."

Gwen said: "Well, I must be going now. I'm rather late as it is." She said to Atwater: "Good-bye."

"Good-bye," said Atwater. He said: "I expect we'll meet again soon." Gwen went away, slamming slightly the door behind her.

"Come and sit on this," said Lola. "Isn't Gwen sweet?"

"Isn't she?"

"She's a darling," said Lola.

She looked more than ever like a very knowing child. Atwater said:

"Are you going to show me some of your posters?"

"Not now. Let's sit here."

Atwater took her hand.

"When did you first notice me at that party?" she said.

"Oh, as soon as you came in."

"I think sometimes people do just feel that at once, don't you?"

"I'm sure they do."

"Are you always falling for people?"

"Yes, always."

"You brute."

"I'm sure everybody falls for you," he said.

"No, they don't."

"I'm sure they do."

In her serious voice she said: "Don't you think sexual selection is awfully important?"

"Of course."

"Don't," she said. "You're hurting. You mustn't do that."

"Where are we going to dine tonight?"

"Anywhere you like."

"Where do you think?"

"Don't," she said. "You're not allowed to do that."

"Why not?"

"Because you're not."

"I shall."

She said: "I'm glad we met. But you must behave."

Slowly, but very deliberately, the brooding edifice of seduction, creaking and incongruous, came into being, a vast Heath Robinson mechanism, dually controlled by them and lumbering gloomily down vistas of triteness. With a sort of heavy-fisted dexterity the mutually adapted emotions of each of them became synchronized, until the unavoidable anti-climax was at hand. Later they dined at a restaurant quite near the flat.

## 10

Pringle walked up and down his studio. He walked
awkwardly, as if he had double-jointed knees and might
fall down at any moment. No tailor could make clothes
to fit him, so he had wisely taken to wearing a sort of
semi-fancy dress having for its main foundation gar-
ments bought in French harbors. The studio was comfortable, with hot and cold water laid on in the corner,
so that you could wash your hands after doing a bit of
painting. Pringle said:

"Ever since I saw the last of Olga I have lost interest
in women."

Atwater said: "What has happened to Olga?"

"I don't know."

"I saw her in the street the other day."

"At the same time I cannot help feeling that they are
in some ways something of a necessity."

"What are?"

"Women."

"Oh."

"Yes. You do without them for a time and then you
find yourself thinking of them again."

"You find that?"

"Not at the moment. I may soon."

"How soon?"

Pringle said: "I don't know. Quite soon, I think." He walked about the room. Atwater said:

"Had you anyone special in mind?"

"No. No one special."

"I liked Olga."

"She was all right for a bit."

Atwater moved his position. He had begun to get cramp in his left leg. Pringle said:

"Why do you fidget so much?"

"This chair."

"It is uncomfortable. I sat in it myself the other evening."

"Very uncomfortable."

"It's Spanish. I picked it up cheap because some of the ornamentation is broken off the top."

"You don't notice it much."

"You don't notice it at all," said Pringle. "Was Olga alone?"

"As far as I know. I only saw her from a bus."

"Someone saw her with a dark man. He had a gold tooth."

"She was alone when I saw her."

"Of course, she may have been going to see him."

"Or coming away."

"Yes. She may well have been coming away."

"She looked as if she might be coming away."

"Anyway," said Pringle, "I'm finished with them for the moment. Occasionally one sees someone who attracts one, but not often. For example, I thought that girl we went to the party with the other night—Harriet Twining, was that her name?—was attractive in a way."

"People go mad about her."

"That's absurd, of course, because she isn't really beautiful at all. But there is a certain attraction."

"She's rather like Olga."

"Not in the least. She hasn't got such a good figure."

"Still, she reminds me of her."

"Quite a different type."

"Oh, no."

Pringle said: "They're absolutely different. You must be mad to suggest that they look alike at all."

"You said the other night that all women looked alike to you now."

"Well, I've changed my mind. I've a perfect right to, haven't I? You're being deliberately annoying."

"Keep your hair on."

"Are you trying to make me angry? You don't succeed in the least. Nothing has happened to make me lose my temper."

"It's all the more ridiculous for you to have done so in that case. You're only angry because I said that Harriet looked like Olga."

Pringle said: "Why on earth should I care whether they look alike or not? I've washed my hands of Olga and I don't know Harriet Twining."

"I should ring her up one of these days," said Atwater.

"Ring who up?"

"Harriet Twining."

"Why?"

"I expect she'd enjoy being taken out by you."

"I don't know where she lives."

"I do."

"Do you know her number?"

"Yes."

"Let me have it before you go," said Pringle. "I might perhaps want it some time. If I give a party, for example."

"I should be very careful of her if I were you."

"I'm quite capable of looking after myself."

"I don't feel at all confident that you are."

"I'm not very interested in your opinions."

"If I give you the telephone number," said Atwater, "I insist on giving you my opinions at the same time. You can take it or leave it."

"I shall take the telephone number and leave the opinions."

"Then you'll live to regret it."

"We shall see."

"Meanwhile, how about your show?"

Pringle said: "They say there aren't enough, so I've got to paint three more pictures by the end of next week."

"You can do that all right."

"Of course I can do it. But it's a bore. Now it's time for me to take my medicine. If I leave it any later I shall probably forget it."

Atwater said: "I saw Barlow the other day. He's having a show in October."

Pringle said: "That girl Sophy is a nice girl. He's lucky to have a girl like that."

"Yes, he's lucky to have a girl like that."

"He ought to marry her, I think."

"Do you?"

"Yes, I think he ought to marry her," said Pringle. He took the cork out of the medicine bottle with his teeth and poured some of the medicine into a china mug with the words "Brighton, 1895," on it. He said:

"I've taken the house in the country l was telling you about. It's near the village where Undershaft used to live."

He put the mug to his lips and, rolling his eyes, gulped down the mixture.

## 11

It was almost dark in the restaurant, with a suggestion of tropics before a typhoon. Wauchop, with two girls at his table, was in the corner. Apart from these, and an actor sitting by himself eating a salad, the room was empty. Atwater and Susan Nunnery took the table by the door. At first sight, Atwater thought one of the girls with Wauchop was Lola, but when she turned her head he saw that she was not so young. Wauchop waved to Susan when they came in and upset his bottle of hock, but the girl who looked like Lola prevented it from falling off the table. Wauchop then put his fingers in his mouth and whistled shrilly. Atwater and Susan sat down, and after some minutes the waiter brought them a menu.

"Not much of a life," said the waiter. "Half-past eight in the morning to half-past twelve at night, seven days a week." He was an oldish man, furrowed with the minor dishonesties of uncounted years.

"Rotten," said Atwater.

"Poor thing," said Susan.

Atwater said: "What would you like to eat?"

"Anything."

"Anything?"

"Oh, yes, anything."

Atwater ordered food.

The waiter said: "That dish takes twenty-five minutes."

Atwater said: "I have my life before me."

The waiter went away, shaking his head.

"What do you do?" she said.

"I'm in a museum."

"May I visit you there?"

Atwater said: "If you let me know when you're coming. There are some special cases that are not shown to the public."

"Are they sweet?"

"Some are."

"I'd love to see them."

"Come in, then."

"I'll ring you up one morning."

"Give me about an hour's notice," said Atwater. "Some of them have to be unwrapped."

It was an appreciable but not utterly unreasonable time before food came and soon after that the wine came too. They ate for a bit. The restaurant was filling up. The tall woman who had given the party came in with several men, most of them wearing mustaches and white ties. She was about forty and very tall and well dressed, but not quite thin enough. She smiled across the room to Susan. Atwater heard the waiter say to the couple sitting behind him:

"It's no use grumbling. We've been getting very good ones, but it's too late for them now."

Susan poured herself out some more wine. She said:

"You're nice. You must come and see me some time.

I live miles away from anywhere with my father. You'll like him."

"Tell me about him."

"He's a curious little man with a walrus mustache."

"What does he do?"

"He's a failure."

"Where does he fail?"

"Oh, he doesn't any longer," she said. "He's a retired failure, you see. You must meet him."

"I'd like to."

Wauchop came over to talk to them. He walked across the room with great care and when he arrived he rested both his hands on the table. He nodded to Atwater and said:

"And how is Susan?"

Atwater said: "I read a lot about you in the evening paper tonight."

Wauchop passed his hand over his forehead.

"You'd hardly believe," he said. "You'd hardly believe how painful that sort of publicity is to a man of my mental make-up. It hurts. It positively hurts."

"I hope you've recovered from the Balkan liqueur."

Wauchop made one of his sweeping movements with his hands.

He turned to Susan and said:

"And when are you going to come to sit for me again, beautiful one?"

"When do you want me to?"

"Why not next week?"

"If you like."

"What about Thursday?"

"Yes."

"Thursday, then."

"The same time as before," she said. "I'll ring you if I find I can't come."

Wauchop bowed to the ground. He had drunk too much hock. They watched him reach his own table unscathed and sit down and put his arms round the two girls. In this position he was able to tilt his chair back in comparative safety.

Atwater said: "We must arrange when you are coming round to the museum."

"When do you think?"

The waiter brought them more food.

Harriet Twining and Arthur Gosling came through the door. Harriet was saying:

"From the time you took I thought you expected me to pay for the taxi."

She was in evening dress and looked quite pleased with herself. When she saw Susan she said: "Hullo, darling. What a pretty suit."

"Harriet, how sweet you're looking."

"My dear, you look so grand."

"How are you, Susan?" said Gosling. He was wearing a double-breasted dinner-jacket. He was a young man who was quite bald and looked like a rather shabby greyhound. He was less pleased than Harriet.

"Why don't you ring me up sometime?" he said. "We haven't been out together for ages."

"I will."

"Do."

"Come on," said Harriet. "See you later, duck."

She made a face and she and Gosling moved over to their table. Atwater saw Wauchop get up and go over to talk to them. Susan said:

"You're a friend of Undershaft's, aren't you?"

"Do you know him?"

"I used to. I hear he won't look at a white woman now."

"He's in New York."

"I must go there."

"I'll take you."

Barlow came into the restaurant. He had his very small hat on and his pipe in his mouth, but not lighted. He said good evening to Susan and to Atwater:

"Somebody said that Julia was here tonight. But I suppose they made a mistake."

"I haven't seen her."

"It doesn't matter. I thought I'd just look in and see if she was here. That's all."

"She may come in later."

"I may look in again later in the evening," said Barlow and went away.

They ate. The food was good.

Atwater watched her out of the corner of his eye. She had small white hands and red nails and there was a heavy bracelet on one of her wrists. She had taken her hat off and hung it on a peg behind her chair. Now that he was sitting on a chair next to her it was more possible to believe in her existence, for in the shadows of this room she had more actuality and although that look of being different did not leave her she seemed less to be extrinsic to her background. Atwater said:

"We might have another bottle of this."

"Will you really show me the special cases?"

"Of course."

He lit her cigarette and said:

"What a pity we have never met till now."

"Now we must make up for it."

"You're so lovely."

She smiled at him.

He said it again that he thought her lovely and he was trying to think of a less pedestrian formula when the woman who had given the party came across the room and said:

"May I talk to you for a moment, Susan. My party are all being so tiresome." She had great big cow-like eyes and looked at them both without smiling.

"This is Mr Atwater," said Susan. "He's going to show me the indecent exhibits in his museum."

Faintly stirred, the tall woman said: "Do you collect, then?"

Atwater said: "I guard some of the national collection."

"How marvelous," she said, rather insincerely. She sat down and Atwater poured her out some wine. Susan said:

"Isn't Harriet looking lovely tonight?"

"But you're looking so well, Susan."

"I'm so fat."

"My dear, *I'm* so fat."

"I shall have to bant."

The tall woman said: "There's a place one can go to just outside Munich. They say it's very good."

"Didn't Mildred go there?"

"It was Mildred's nerves."

"Doesn't he do that too?"

"Mildred went to the man at Versailles. He makes you scrub floors. It's a six-months' course and prohibitively expensive. Mildred said she felt quite different after it."

"Then there are readings from Croce in the evening. It's terrible if you don't understand Italian. You're made to listen just the same."

Atwater said: "Is it for both sexes?"

The tall woman said: "I could find that out from Mildred if you thought of going." She looked at him with no interest, through big watery eyes.

"I don't think I will."

Susan said: "Yes, you must."

One of the men who were sitting at the table that the tall woman had left got up and came across the room. He was about the same age as the tall woman and, like her, his clothes fitted very well. He was dark and had bags under the eyes and rather a thick nose, but the general effect was not bad and he hardly looked like a Jew at all. His mustache was arranged so that it made him look as if he might be in the Brigade of

Guards, but although it was plausible it was not really convincing. At the same time it was carried off well enough and did not seem silly. He said to the tall woman:

"Why have you left us?"

"This is Mr Verelst," she said. "But you know Susan, don't you?"

"I think we've met before."

"Of course we have."

"May I sit down for a moment?" said Verelst.

"Do," Atwater said. "Waiter, bring another glass."

Screams came from Wauchop's table. One of the girls with him, a model, was having hysterics. She was a good-looking girl with an ugly mouth and she laughed and laughed until it became a sort of sobbing. Wauchop and the other girl who looked like Lola laughed too, but not so loud. The tall woman said:

"Wauchop is enjoying himself tonight."

Verelst said: "For a short time we were in the same company during the war."

"What was he like then?" Atwater said.

"Much the same as he is now. Only, of course, you were shot for desertion if you made him an excuse for leaving the country."

Susan said: "I like my Wauchop. You only talk like that cause you are jealous of him, both of you."

"He's all right," said Verelst. "You get shell-shock if you're with him long. But he's all right."

"They say he's going to marry one of those girls," said the tall woman.

Verelst sat there and watched Susan. He looked rather distinguished, but his clothes fitted him too well in the wrong way and the bags under his eyes made him seem more tired than he really was. He watched Susan for a little and then said:

"It's absurd that we haven't met for so long."

"Yes. Isn't it?"

"You must come out with me," he said. He said to Atwater:

"It's so rude, my coming and sitting at your table in this way. I'll hope you'll forgive me."

The tall woman said: "We were talking about that place where Mildred went for her nerves."

Verelst said: "They forced her to make beds all the time, didn't they?"

But he wasn't really interested in what they had done to Mildred. He said to Susan:

"Do you still live in the same place?"

"In the book. Under George Nunnery."

Verelst said to Atwater: "How clever of you to know that this is the only possible wine to drink here." He had good manners and left off looking at Susan while he talked to Atwater.

Atwater said: "I thought it seemed a bit heavier than usual tonight."

Verelst said: "Of course, you ought to go to where it comes from. I stayed near there for some time a year or two go."

"Really?"

"If you ever thought of going I could give you the address of a really excellent hotel. It's food that can compare with anywhere in Europe that I know of."

"Do give me the address before you go."

"I will," said Verelst. "Of course the place is always full of international gourmets, if you can stand that." He said to Susan: "I shall ring you up, then."

"Do."

The tall woman said: "It must have done Mildred a great deal of good to do things like scrubbing floors. She was always a bundle of nerves."

Atwater said: "Do you know many people who have gone there."

The tall woman said: "Of course it's not everyone who can afford it."

Barlow came in again. He said to Atwater:

"I suppose there's been no sign of Julia?"

"No. No sign."

Barlow was still wearing his hat, but he was carrying his pipe in his hand.

"She must have gone somewhere else," he said. "In that case I shall retire to bed." He went away.

Harriet and Gosling came over from their table. Harriet said:

"May we join you if we bring our bottle. It isn't anything like finished." She was carrying the bottle in the bucket, and put the bucket on the table. Gosling said:

"You can't hear yourself speak over there, Wauchop is making such a noise."

"Do you know everybody?" said Atwater. He hoped

that lots more people would come and talk and drink and sit at the table and make assignations with Susan and give him good advice and argue with each other, because then it would become funny and he might feel less angry. The tall woman said to Harriet:

"Wasn't it a friend of yours who lay on the floor for such a long time at my party?"

Harriet said: "Why, of course it was. I'd forgotten all about him. He's rather an old sweet really. He's called Scheigan. He's an American publisher and he's going to do my book when it's finished."

"Americans always have such a lot of misdirected party spirit," said Gosling. "One came to a party I gave two years ago and drank so much that he died soon after."

"It was probably the drink you gave him," said Harriet. "I've never known anyone like you. You seem to think that people will drink anything."

"Most of them will. Anyway, you've nothing to grumble at tonight. It was a very good bottle of wine indeed."

"You know I hate champagne. Why, because it's your birthday, I should be made to drink it is more than I can imagine."

"You never need do it again. It makes you much too bad-tempered."

The tall woman said: "Did you say that the man who lay on the floor at my party died soon after?"

"Oh, no, he's not dead, is he?" said Harriet. "Or is he? Of course he's not very young."

Atwater said: "He's not dead, unless he fell out of the taxi on the way back."

Verelst said: "Why wasn't I asked to this party of yours?"

"Because I didn't think that sort of party amused you."

Harriet said: "I hope old Scheigan isn't dead. Did I tell you his Christian name is Marquis?"

Gosling said : "It's my American who died. Not yours."

"Who do you call your American?"

The one who came to my party."

"Oh, the one you poisoned with bad drink."

Atwater wished that they were all in hell. The evening continued. Gosling ordered another bottle of something. They talked. Verelst said:

"I shall have to go now. I've got a car outside. Can I give anyone a lift?" He glanced at Susan but just the right amount, so that the invitation was given without being at all pressing. She said:

"Good night. Ring me up some time."

"And by the way," said Verelst to Atwater, "if you've got a pencil I could give you the address of that hotel."

"I'm afraid I haven't got one."

"Never mind," said Verelst. "I expect we shall meet again soon. If not, I can get your address from Susan and send it to you."

Atwater said: "I dare say one of the waiters has got a pencil."

"Anyway, I can easily send it to you. I'll do that."

"Good night."

"Good night."

The tall woman said: "I suppose I ought to go back to my party now. I hope you haven't minded my sitting with you all this time."

She got up and said good-bye with limp affection. Susan got up too.

"You're not going, are you?" said Harriet.

Susan said: "Yes, I'm tired. Anyway, the place will close soon." She said to Atwater: "You must take me home now."

She put on her hat. Harriet said to Gosling:

"Where do you think it would be fun to go now?"

Atwater began to sort out from his bill some of the bottles of wine ordered by other people. He said to the waiter:

"About these two glasses of maraschino?"

"Maraschino?"

"Yes."

"Come to think of it," said the waiter, "I believe some-one had them last night."

They picked up a taxi outside. Susan told the driver where to go. In the taxi she said:

"No, don't be a bore. I'm tired."

It was, as she had said, miles away. The taxi turned south just before they reached Olympia and stopped in front of a house with a decayed outside. The place had been turned into flats. The front door was not locked. They pushed it open and went up the stairs. It was pitch dark and the stairs smelled horribly.

"We go up to the top," said Susan.

She took his hand. They climbed several flights of rather narrow stairs. Quite a lot of things had been left about on the stairs and they fell over some of them. When they arrived at the top she turned on the light. The air was noticeably more fresh on the top landing.

"This is it."

"Oh, is it?"

They stood there for a few seconds and she held his hand. There was suddenly a great deal of noise below them. Someone else was coming up the stairs. They too were falling over the things left about on the stairs. The collisions echoed up to the top landing.

"Who is this?"

"My father."

"Where has he been?"

"Party."

They listened to Mr Nunnery coming up the stairs. On the landing below them they heard him stop and say "Curses." He ran up the last flight of stairs very fast and only just managed to round the corner without falling down. He now appeared in sight. He was wearing a dinner jacket.

"Hullo, Susan," he said.

"Hullo."

"I've been to a lovely party," said Mr Nunnery. "*Lovely.*"

"This is Mr Atwater," said Susan. "I've been having dinner with him."

"Come in," said Mr Nunnery. "Come in and have a

drink. I think there's some whisky left. Anyway, we can see."

"No, it's too late," said Susan, "and I'm tired. You go off to bed."

Mr Nunnery said: "My daughter is very inhospitable. I hope she has not been in this mood all the evening. She's like this at times. I suppose I must wish you good night."

"Good night," said Atwater.

"Good night," said Mr Nunnery, "good night."

"Nasty old man," said Susan. "You must meet him some other time. You'll like him."

They heard Mr Nunnery crashing about inside the flat. Atwater said:

"I thought he was so nice."

"Good night, darling," she said. "And thank you so much for dinner."

"Good night," said Atwater.

## 12

Recognizing Nosworth by his walk, fast even after lunch, Atwater hurried after him, but did not catch him up until he had turned the corner. When he saw Atwater, Nosworth said:

"I'm going to Raymond Pringle's show."

"So am I."

"I disliked his father a great deal. I once had to sit next to him at a public dinner in Manchester. I shall be interested to see what they are like."

They walked on together until they came to the gallery. Pringle never had much difficulty in getting shows as there was a small but obstinate public that bought his pictures, never enough to satisfy Pringle himself and only just enough to make it worth the gallery's while to give him another show, but never deserting him entirely.

"No," said Nosworth, "I don't want a catalogue," to the man at the door, an ape-faced dotard in uniform, who fussed unsteadily towards them as they came in, bent on causing some petty annoyance. The gallery was almost empty as it was lunch time. The young man in charge of it had only just come back from lunch himself and he stood there in his black hat talking to two old women. Atwater, as he walked round, heard one of the three say: "Uccello or Utrillo?" Nosworth passed quickly from picture to picture, saying to himself:

"Oh dear, oh dear..."

Atwater had seen most of the pictures before, but he walked round with Nosworth because he was still uncertain as to the identity of some of the models and was glad to have the opportunity of reinvestigating the matter with the pictures in a fresh setting. The two old women went away and the young man in charge of the gallery took off his hat and, sitting down at a side table, began to sort press cuttings. There were only a few people in the gallery. Nosworth said:

"It does not seem to be a very popular private view. However, I see one or two of them have been sold."

"It will fill up soon. Everybody is having lunch."

The young man in charge of the gallery put a pin through the corner of a bunch of cuttings and threw them into a tray lying on his table. He yawned. Then he got up and came across the room. He said to Nosworth:

"I don't know whether you're interested in modern art at all. It's funny sort of stuff. When you first see it you hardly know what to make of it. It looks as if the thing is hung upside down or something. Then after a bit you get the hang of it."

"Thank you," said Nosworth. "My friend explains the pictures to me."

"That's an interesting one over there."

"In what way?"

"The recession is very ably handled."

Nosworth looked at the picture intently and then looked away into the gallery's middle distance.

"It's a little place near Marseilles," said the young man. "I've been there."

"Have you?"

"There are some of the artist's drawings here, if you'd care to see them."

"Not today, thank you."

"We've got lots of interesting pictures here," said the young man. "All the moderns, you know. And all the others too for that matter. Everything, really."

Nosworth said: "Some other time you must show them all to me. All of them. As it happens, I am in a great hurry at the present moment and must in fact be going, at once."

The young man leaned against the wall with his hands in his pockets.

"Any time," he said. "You'll like them."

He was not listening when Nosworth said: "I venture to suggest that it is for me to say what I like. Not you."

Nosworth sat down on a chair and looked straight in front of him. He did not speak. Atwater looked at pictures by painters other than Pringle, one or two of which had been left about the gallery. Pringle himself came in, bothered and angry.

"Hullo," he said to Atwater. He said to the young man in charge:

"Any more sold?"

"I think I shall be able to place *Girl's Torso*."

"Who?"

"I'm afraid we're not at liberty to tell you."

"Oh, aren't we?" said Pringle. "Well, while you're

here, which I noticed you weren't most of the morning, what about the catalogue?"

"What about it?"

"It reads like a collection of schoolboy howlers."

The young man said: "You didn't let us have the list in time for us to see a proof and I couldn't read your writing myself."

He walked away, scratching the seat of his trousers moodily, and sat down again at his table. People were beginning to come into the gallery. Atwater said:

"Did you have a crowd this morning?"

Pringle said: "Not so bad." But he was too fussed to talk to anyone and he wandered up and down, twitching. Nosworth said:

"I shall have to be getting back soon."

More people came into the gallery. Lola came in. She was wearing a cloak and a brightly colored duster round her neck. She saw Atwater at once and said:

"I've just come in for a moment. I've got to fly."

"So have I."

"Why?"

"I've got to go back and work."

"Can't you come to a cinema with me?"

"No."

"Why not?"

"I've got to work."

"You're coming to see me this evening, aren't you?"

"Yes, of course I am."

"These are very striking, aren't they?" she said, meaning Pringle's pictures.

"Very striking."

"Don't they remind you of somebody?"

"Everybody."

The gallery was getting quite full. There was rather a tense feeling in the air as if no one was very sure of themselves. All Pringle's acquaintances were there and one or two journalists he had quarreled with. Pringle himself was so edgy that it was impossible to talk to him, so he stood in the corner of the room and bit his nails. Barlow, Verelst, and Mr Scheigan came through the door almost at the same moment. Mr Scheigan bought a catalogue. Barlow stood and looked round the room and then came across to Atwater. He said:

"Raymond seems to have collected quite a presentable crowd."

He took a good look at Lola. Atwater introduced them.

While they were talking, Pringle came away from the corner he had been standing in and said to Atwater:

"I sent Harriet Twining a card for this. Do you think she will come?"

"You never know."

Atwater did not think it very likely. He heard Barlow say: "Why don't you come round and see me some time?" and Lola give her telephone number. Pringle said:

"Not that I care in the least whether she comes or not. But I thought I'd just send her a card."

Lola said to Atwater: "Well, I must be going now. I've got an appointment."

"Good-bye."

"I shall see you this evening," she said. She went out, readjusting the duster. Barlow said:

"You'll never get rid of that girl."

"Are you going to make me an offer?"

"No," said Barlow, "I don't think so."

The crowd was thick and they were all talking. Atwater said:

"Do you know the name of that dark man over there who came in just in front of you?"

"Verelst. He buys pictures sometimes."

They watched Mr Scheigan making his way round the room. He was trying to look at the pictures as if there was no private view going on and it took him a long time to get round. As he passed them Barlow said:

"Hullo, Mr Scheigan."

"Mr Barlow!" said Mr Scheigan. "This is great."

"Fancy meeting you here."

"I'm just crazy about pictures."

"You are?"

"When I was over in Paris in the fall," said Mr Scheigan, "I gave thirty thousand francs for a picture that wasn't half the size of any of this lot here."

Atwater said: "This is the man who painted them. He can do small ones too."

He caught Pringle, who was moving in dejection through the crowd, by the arm.

"Glad to meet you, Mr Pringle," said Mr Scheigan. "It's a grand show you've got here."

Pringle said: "I hope you didn't feel too bad after the

other night." It always annoyed him when people did not recognize him. Mr Scheigan said:

"That little party the other night didn't worry old man Scheigan. Nobody knows how to throw a party over here. But I'll give your folks credit for one thing. They knew my little weakness when they sent me the card that admits here."

Barlow said: "You're a connoisseur."

Mr Scheigan said: "I love art. I just can't live without it."

"You can't?"

"I'm like that somehow."

"Don't worry. We won't hurt you. You're among friends."

Pringle looked as if he would like to sell Mr Scheigan something pretty expensive, but he did not say anything. Barlow said:

"I've got some art too that you might like to come round and see one of these days."

"Are you a painter, Mr Barlow?"

Barlow said he was. Mr Scheigan said: "That's great. And you, Mr Atwater?"

"No, I'm not, I'm afraid."

"Well," said Mr Sheigan, "we can't all make beauty, but we publishers are men with a frustrated creative urge. Maybe we don't always do noble things, but we dream them all day long."

"Do you?"

"I'll say we do," said Mr Scheigan.

Barlow said: "You don't do yourself justice, Mr

Scheigan. But let's go out and have a drink on the strength of it. Can you leave this room, Raymond?"

Pringle said: "I'm expecting somebody."

"William?"

"I must go back and work."

"Well, if you won't, you won't," said Barlow. "But I expect Mr Scheigan and I may do so later."

Nosworth still sat on the chair, but several people who knew him had arrived who stood round him in a circle hiding him from view. Verelst, who had been talking to the young man in charge of the gallery, strolled across the room. He looked even less like a Jew than he had done the night before. He was very smartly dressed. Atwater noticed how well his shoes were made. Verelst said:

"We meet again."

"How are you?" said Atwater. He introduced Pringle. Verelst said:

"I see red labels everywhere."

Pringle said: "Most of them on ones that have been lent."

He was gloomy and had nerves. He went on biting his nails.

"They seem very well hung," said Verelst. He evidently thought that it was a rotten show but was prepared to be polite about it. Pringle always knew by instinct when anyone did not like his pictures. They produced a recognizable reaction on him. He would take great trouble with them and the more hopeless it appeared to be to win them over the more he would insist on their examining the detail of his technique. They were the only people he took any open pleasure in showing his pictures to. If possible, he would try and persuade them to sit for their portraits, but today he seemed too gloomy to apply himself to the conversion of Verelst and he only said:

"You see most of them best from this end of the room."

Verelst said: "Yes, the light falls rather badly by the door." He said to Atwater:

"That was a very pleasant party we had last night."

"Wasn't it?"

"I expect you know Susan well. I see her so rarely. She's so difficult to get hold of."

"She's full of engagements."

"As a matter of fact, she's coming out with me next week," said Verelst. "But it will be the first time for ages."

"Oh, will it?"

"Ages. I think only once before, anyway. And then only because we were going to the same party, or something like that, after."

"You've known her for a long time?"

"Oh no. I met her some little time ago and then I went abroad, so I was glad to run into you both last night."

"One meets everyone there, of course."

"Everyone."

The young man in charge of the gallery came up to them very suddenly and said to Verelst:

"Then there's another I could probably get from a

private source. It's a lovely one. Bernheim was after it."

"Splendid," said Verelst. "Write to me about it."

"I'll try to get a photograph of it."

"Do you buy many pictures?" said Atwater.

Verelst said: "You must come and see them some time. Unfortunately, most of them are stored."

"Then I'll send you a letter," said the gallery young man.

Verelst said: "Yes. Put it in writing." He did the big collector and eccentric nobleman stuff well in the circumstances but with a little too much unconcern. He said to Atwater:

"Will you come and lunch with me one of these days?"

"I'd like to very much."

Nosworth got up from his chair and pushed his way through the crowd of people who were talking to him. He said:

"I don't want to see any more pictures now. Besides, I have to give an interview to a Czech."

"I must go too," said Atwater. "Good-bye," he said to Verelst.

"Good-bye," said Verelst. "You must come and lunch with me and I'll give you that address I told you about last night."

Barlow said: "Haven't you time to have one with Mr Scheigan and me?"

"I can't."

"Why, you're not going, Mr Atwater?" said Mr Scheigan. "When are you boys coming round to see me?"

"Come on," said Barlow. "If we don't make haste they'll be shut."

"Shut?" said Mr Scheigan. "Why will they be shut?"

"I can't explain now," said Barlow. "You must take my word for it. I may look in again, Raymond."

He and Mr Scheigan went out. Nosworth and Atwater followed, but more slowly. As they passed the young man in charge of the gallery Nosworth said:

"Good day."

The senile cretin at the door muttered toothlessly: "Taxi, sir?" and leered. It was full of sun outside as they walked up the street.

Nosworth said: "We might really bus back to the museum. I appear to be a little late already."

"Is he an important Czech?"

Nosworth nodded. He said:

"Who was the man you were talking to?"

"He's called Verelst."

"Oh yes," said Nosworth. "He's got one or two very nice things."

"Do you know anything about him?"

"He collects things."

"What else?"

"I suppose he's a Jew, isn't he?"

"I suppose so."

The bus passed through back streets, avoiding where the road was being repaired. When they got back to the museum they found that the Czech had been waiting for some time. He was a meek-looking man, but was too intent on his subject to talk to in any sort of comfort. After being introduced to Nosworth, he said:

"*Etes-vous professeur?*"

"*Non.*"

"*Pourquoi pas?*"

Nosworth said: "*Parce que c'est trop difficile.*"

The Czech sat down and began to take a number of papers from a shiny black case which he had brought with him. Nosworth looked at the Czech thoughtfully. Atwater sat down at his own desk.

## 13

Speaking of Pringle to Atwater in the course of a fairly general disquisition on the ups and downs of himself and his friends, Barlow said:

"Of course he was intended by nature to be gold-dug and, as a compensation, given a temperament that enjoys the process."

"Olga?"

"And now Olga has gone it will be someone else."

Barlow put his fork into the spaghetti on his plate and twisted it round and round so that it clung knotted about the prongs. Then he forced it into his mouth. He said:

"His show is doing very well. I only hope mine will do as well in the autumn."

"Did you do anything with Scheigan?"

"He wanted to take two things away and send me the money from America when he got back, as his draft on the bank over here wasn't big enough."

"Did you do it?"

"In the end he took a drawing and gave me a pound for it on account."

"He's open-handed."

"He can't resist beauty," said Barlow; "he told me he couldn't."

"How is he getting on with Harriet?"

"She won't come near him. She's got his gold cigarette case. He's very upset."

"Harriet is a smart girl."

"Harriet is a nice girl," said Barlow. "But she's a bit too clever for me."

"How is Sophy?"

"Sophy has gone out of London to see her sister. It makes a change for both of us."

"Then you think Raymond has fallen for Harriet?"

"I hope it stops him from ringing up Sophy all day long. I'm not afraid that he'll take her away from me, but I don't like it."

"Does he ring her up often?"

Barlow said: "No, I don't think so. But I'm not sure." He said: "Was it you dining with Susan Nunnery the other night?"

"Yes."

"She's a nice girl," said Barlow. "Not my sort. But nice."

"I like her."

Barlow said: "Waiter, a black coffee—will you have a black coffee?—two black coffees, and I shall have a cheap cigar. Let me see what you've got." He said: "What I really wanted to talk to you about was not women but the picture that Naomi Race picked up the other day."

"It's not bad."

"Good condition?"

Atwater said: "A trifle *sfumato*. Rather in the manner of Valdès."

## 14

Atwater sat in the downstairs room where the bar was. He sat on a high stool eating chips. The barman said:

"What's yours, sir?"

Atwater could not remember whether the barman's name was George or John. He said:

"I'm waiting for someone."

The bar was empty except for two young men, who sat at the other end of the bar and looked like perhaps quietly dressed pimps. One of these said:

"It was those perished valve rubbers that started the trouble. I saw that at once."

The other one said: "You've said it," and to the barman:

"How's George today?"

"How's yourself, sir?"

The first one said: "That was a good one you mixed for me on Thursday, captain."

"One of our specials, sir?"

"That Old Etonian."

"It's a good cocktail, sir."

"I should think it was a good cocktail, George."

"Feel a bit lit after it, sir?"

The young man leant across the bar, and said:

"I'll tell you this, George. I was squiffy after two of them. It's a fact."

He said it confidentially, as one might say: "The gift of tongues descended on me last night after months of fasting." Atwater ate chips. An elderly man wearing a puce tie came into the bar. He had a slightly military look. By his appearance he might once have held a commission in some Balkan army medical corps. He stared round the bar.

"What's it to be this evening, sir?" said the barman.

"Make it one of the usual," said the elderly man. He sat down and glanced at Atwater.

"How's business, George?" said one of the young men.

"We mustn't grumble, sir."

The barman applied himself to moving about objects that were out of sight underneath the bar. The elderly man fidgeted on his stool and sipped his drink. He said to Atwater:

"A trifle cooler this evening."

"Just a little."

"Could you pass me the olives?"

Atwater moved the olives and the chips and the salted almonds and the matches over and ordered a Martini. The elderly man said:

"I think we've met before, haven't we?"

"I don't think so."

"Well, perhaps not."

"I don't seem to remember it."

"Will you have a drink?"

"Thank you. I've just ordered one."

"Have another?"

"I won't, thanks. I'm waiting for someone."

Atwater ate chips. The elderly man went away. It was only a temporary absence, because he left his drink unfinished and beside it on the bar a pair of lavender gloves. He also left a rather tattered copy of a paper bound book called *L'Ersatz d'amour.* Atwater wondered whether Susan was going to make him wait all night in the bar. The two young men had another round.

"Happy days," one of them said.

The other said: "Here's how."

The first one said: "Fact is, you must always be keeping an eye on valves."

"That's so."

The elderly man returned. He moved his stool along the bar. He lit a cigarette and offered one to Atwater, who refused it with thanks. He said:

"It looks as if your friend is not going to come."

"Women think it their duty to keep one waiting."

"Oh, it's a woman, is it?"

"Yes," said Atwater, "it's a woman."

The elderly man cleared his throat with almost offensive delicacy.

Atwater sipped his drink. The elderly man said:

"Ever go to the cinema?"

Atwater said: "Hardly ever. I'm funny that way."

He wondered why he had not taken the trouble to buy an evening paper to read. Or was she not going to turn up at all? The two young men finished their second round. They climbed down from their stools.

"So long, skipper."

"Good evening, sir."

"Be good, George."

"The same to you, sir. Good evening, sir."

Atwater drank his Martini. He would have liked another, but the alternatives seemed to be buying a drink for the man in the puce tie or allowing the man in the puce tie to buy one for him. He felt a disinclination from both these courses. He sat. The barman began to wash glasses. After drying each one, he held it up to the light and examined it intently as if to make sure that the liquids poured into it had not corroded the surface of the glass.

"Are you interested in motoring at all?" said the man in the puce tie.

"Negligibly," said Atwater. Was the girl ever going to turn up? He supposed she wasn't. The elderly man said that he often went for long motor drives on Sundays. He found it gave him an appetite. Atwater ate chips. The barman retired to the far end of the bar. He began reading an evening paper that he had folded up into a very small neat packet. The elderly man took a deep breath. He said:

"It's getting late."

"It is."

"Do you mind if I speak plainly?"

"Yes," said Atwater, "I do. I should hate it. George, I want another Martini."

"Dry, sir?"

"Dry."

Two girls and a young man came into the bar. They

sat down at a table. One of the girls said:

"I made her kneel in front of me and apologize."

She was a plump little thing, wearing a Gunner tie, and she looked as if she meant what she said. The other girl said:

"A few months' happiness, a few weeks even, you've got to be glad of."

"Live and let live, that's what I say," said the young man. He pulled the lapels of his double-breasted coat so that it fitted well into his shoulders and went to the bar and ordered two Clover Clubs and a Sidecar. Somewhere outside the room the telephone began to ring. A waiter came in.

"Mr Water?" he said. "Any gentleman of that name?"

"Yes," said Atwater, "possibly."

"Wanted on the phone," said the waiter. He said to the barman: "Neronian wasn't placed."

"You didn't go and back it?"

"Sure thing."

"Go on."

The waiter said: "That horse will be a second Tishy, not half."

The barman said: "You'll make more money by keeping it in your pocket next time."

The waiter wiped his mouth with the back of his hand. Atwater went outside to the telephone. He took up the receiver. Susan's voice sounded very far away. She said:

"So sorry I shan't be able to see you tonight. I'm in the country."

"I see."

"I can't get away."

"Can't you?"

"You don't mind, do you?"

"Yes."

She laughed.

"No, you don't really."

"All right, I don't."

She said: "I feel an awful little bitch about this."

Atwater said: "No, that's all right."

"I do really."

"These things will happen."

She laughed again.

"Good-bye," she said.

"Good-bye."

She said: "Ring me up soon."

Atwater hung up the receiver. The elderly man in the puce tie passed on his way out. He said:

"Good night. We must meet again some time."

Atwater went back into the room where the bar was. Two Martinis seemed to have made a pleasantly light dinner, but as he had the evening before him he ate a plate of bacon and eggs in the corner of the room. When he had eaten the bacon and eggs he rang up a few people he knew, all of whom were out or did not answer the telephone. The club showed no signs of filling up. It was getting late. Atwater decided that the only thing to do was to call on Nosworth. Nosworth had never taken the trouble to have the telephone installed, but he would almost certainly be in.

It was raining outside. In Charing Cross Road, Atwater took a bus, jumping on as it slowed down to pass some taxis. He wondered whether Susan was having fun in the country. He thought that after all the country couldn't be much fun in this weather. On the other hand, the weather might not be the same in the country. The bus went along Tottenham Court Road and turned round in the direction of King's Cross. Nosworth lived in the several attics of a large house in north-east Bloomsbury. Atwater got off the bus and turned up a side street. The rain had stopped now but the pavements were still shining with water. Atwater rang the caretaker's bell, and was let in. He went up the stairs and knocked on Nosworth's door. Nosworth opened the door himself. He was wearing only a pair of evening trousers and a long-sleeved porridge-colored vest.

"Come in," he said.

Atwater said: "Are you going out?"

"I have to go to a reception given for that Czech," said Nosworth. "I've just had a shockingly bad dinner at Pavesi's."

"May I stay while you dress?"

Nosworth said: "There appear to be some peculiar stains on my white waistcoat. It would not do for me to wear a black one, do you think?"

"Hardly."

"It's unfashionable."

"Yes."

The room was mostly filled with books. There was a shapeless piece of stone in one corner, excavated from

Asia Minor and said to represent Diana of the Ephesians. Atwater said:

"I've just been put off dinner at the last moment."

"A woman, of course," said Nosworth. "I suppose I ought to wear suspenders?"

"Oh yes."

"Are you very angry?"

"Very."

"I used to be just the same," said Nosworth. "But the older I got the more insistent I became on qualities that no woman has ever, nor could ever, possess. The elastic seems to have perished since I last wore these."

"What happened?"

Nosworth said: "Well, I never see any of them now. When I'm over there I sometimes go to a place I know in the rue de Liège, but I always feel it's waste of money. Give me my white tie, will you? It's in the top small drawer. I'm afraid it's not very clean. I must have forgotten to send it to the wash after the archbishops' dinner."

Nosworth pinned on his medals. He brushed some of the dust off his trousers. He said:

"Of course, some people think that the only cure for women is more women."

Atwater said: "I know that is a theory."

"It's not one I hold myself."

"Don't you?"

"These evening clothes are a bit the worse for wear, don't you think?"

"Possibly."

"But they'll do."

"Oh yes."

"I got them in Athens before the war. They were a disgraceful price, but I must say they have lasted very well. Have I forgotten something?"

"Your key?"

"Yes," said Nosworth. "My key. As I'm a little early and I have nothing to offer you here, shall we look in at the Plumbers' Arms as we pass? I don't want to arrive too soon."

It had begun to rain again when they got out into the street. Outside the Plumbers' Arms a man was playing the cornet. He was playing *Ah! Sweet Mystery of Life*. Later he came into the saloon bar with a small velvet bag and collected money. Nosworth dropped several half-pennies into the bag.

"I must be going," Nosworth said. They went out and Atwater made his way home through the rain.

Lola said: "Hullo, William."

She always used a surprised voice when Atwater arrived, as if she had not expected to see him, even if he had been speaking to her on the telephone ten minutes before and had said that he was already on his way to see her.

"You never come and see me," she said.

Atwater sat down. He looked round the room at the little bits of watered silk hung round the walls. "I must have color," Lola used to say. She lay on the divan. She said:

"Why do you never come to see me?"

"But here I am."

"You never come."

"Whenever I have a moment."

"You treat me very badly."

Atwater said: "Men do treat women badly. You must have discovered that by now."

The toastingfork was lying on the table and he picked it up and struck her with it once or twice, but not hard. Then he went and sat beside her on the divan while she talked for a time about his never coming to see her.

"Where's Gwen?"

"She's gone away for the weekend."

"Oh."

"She doesn't like you."

"I know she doesn't."

"What are you going to do about it?"

"Nothing."

And then art. She talked about that for some time. Or, alternatively, literature. Atwater smoked.

"Who was the man you introduced me to at that private view?"

"Hector Barlow?"

"He's so attractive."

"Is he?"

"Don't you think?"

"I don't know."

The divan creaked. Lola said:

"No, dear, no."

"Yes."

"No, really, no."

"Yes."

"Draw the curtains, then."

As Atwater drew the curtains he noticed that it was spotting with rain outside and in one of the back rooms opposite a man wearing an overcoat was playing the piano. Lola said:

"In modern sculpture I think the influence of Archipenko is paramount."

Barlow said: "If it's really poisoning your life, why not ask her to marry you? I sometimes do that. Girls like it. Besides, you'd be quite safe. I don't expect she'd accept you for a moment. The other thing to do would be to get the museum to advance you a quarter's salary and take her down to Brighton for the weekend. But I don't expect she'd do that either. She's got other fish to fry."

Atwater said: "Brighton air gives me a liver."

"Then you'll have to marry her," said Barlow. "Having old Nunnery for a father-in law would make the trouble and expense almost worth while."

On his way out of the museum Atwater passed
Nosworth, arguing in the evening sunshine with a party
of Negroes, who stood about him in ungainly positions,
near in spirit to the Anglo-Saxon attitudes of First Mes-
senger.

"If you come here," Nosworth was sayings "you must
obey the regulations. No smoking. It is written up as
plainly as anything can be."

He did not answer when Atwater said good night.

Atwater went towards the Underground station. The
trains were crowded, because he had come out of the
museum late and it was the rush hour. He wondered
what having cocktails at Susan's would be like. The
train was very full of people and he had to stand all the
way. As usual, the denaturalized light made some of
the women traveling look rather beautiful. Atwater considered them, but in a detached way. He walked quickly
out of the train, and was the first to reach the lift, but
this did not make any difference with regard to arriv-
ing at the party any sooner, because the lift man waited
until everyone had come off the train and into the lift
before he started. When the lift was at ground level he
opened the farther gate. Atwater walked out. The flat
was not far from the station. The outside door of the
house was open and there was a notice on it telling

guests to come upstairs. The staircase still smelled bad, but a number of the larger objects had been cleared away from it so that it was easier to walk up it. About halfway up he began to hear the gramophone. The door was open when he came to the top of the stairs and Atwater went in and put his hat under the table in the hall. Susan was standing by the door holding a cocktail shaker in her hand.

"Hullo, darling."

"Hullo," said Atwater.

"Have a drink," she said.

She gave him a drink. It was not very strong and quite nasty. Then she went to the other side of the room and gave someone else a drink. Atwater looked round the room. There were a lot of people in it, about half of whom he knew by sight. Mr Nunnery was leaning against the mantelpiece, drinking something out of a tumbler. He was talking to Fotheringham. Atwater moved through the crowd towards them. Mr Nunnery blinked and nodded. He evidently did not remember that he had met Atwater before, but he seemed very friendly. Before Atwater could speak Fotheringham held up his hand and said:

"My dear William, forgive me if I just finish this conversation, but it affects my whole career. Then I have something that I want to say to you." He turned to Mr Nunnery and said:

"What would you quote me for National Incorporated, for instance?"

Mr Nunnery took a deep breath. He said:

"That is a question I should not be prepared to answer on the spur of the moment." He said to Atwater:

"If you can't drink that stuff, there's some whisky over there."

"And then mines?" said Fotheringham.

"To the technical mind, mines present all manner of difficulties."

Fotheringham said: "Did I tell you, William, that I was thinking of changing my job?"

"I think so."

"I can't have done. I've only just made up my mind."

"America?"

"Oh yes. Well, I may have to postpone America for a year or two. I was talking to Mr Nunnery about the City. He thinks I might do well there."

Mr Nunnery said: "There's no doubt there's money to be made there. And money to be lost too."

Fotheringham said: "I think I should make money. Granted I have no experience and no head for figures. But I think I have *flair*. I can tell from the names whether shares are going up or not. I always keep an eye on the financial columns and I find I'm usually right."

"But does that hold good over an extended period? That's the important point."

"It may sound absurd," said Fotheringham, "and all that, but if you gave me twenty thousand pounds I guarantee to double it for you by the end of the year."

Mr Nunnery said: "It's a great pity we can't go into partnership together. Between us, with my experience and your initiative, we might do some good."

His eyes, which were filmy, brightened up a little. He had perhaps been good looking as a young man, but he did not resemble Susan at all. He said to Atwater:

"I don't expect you're very interested in finance?"

"I don't know much about it."

"It's an absorbing occupation," said Mr Nunnery. "Too absorbing, really. It leaves you no time to lead your own life. That was one of the reasons I gave it up. The other was because I had no more money."

"But that's the whole point," said Fotheringham. "I have no money. Therefore I go into the City."

Mr Nunnery said: "With me it was different. I had none. Therefore I left it. It's purely a question of mental attitude."

"But what do you really think?"

"It's an idea you ought to give careful consideration to."

"I think so too," said Fotheringham. "Now what I wanted to ask you, William, was, in the event of my not becoming a captain of industry, could your museum arrange to send me out on an expedition somewhere?"

"Where?"

"Oh, anywhere. That's immaterial really. Sumatra or Guyana. Somewhere where they collect specimens."

"I'll mention your name if I should hear of anything."

"I wish you would. The fact is, I do feel a cut above my present job. It doesn't give me scope."

"The really able seldom reach the top of the tree," said Mr Nunnery. "Jealousy and so on."

Fotheringham said: "I wouldn't go so far as to describe myself as one of the Really Able. But I don't like seeing what qualities I have wasted."

Atwater watched Susan, who was standing on the other side of the room with Verelst. She was balancing the cocktail shaker on the palm of her hand and was listening to some story he was telling and looked at Verelst with her eyes very wide open. Verelst was leaning against the wall, not so well dressed as usual and evidently having gone to bed late the night before. It made him seem older. Susan had her head a little on one side. Verelst was telling the story well, using his hands, but not at all as if he wanted to sell something. Only he looked as if it would hurt him if she did not hear every word that he was saying to her. When you were close to him you could see that he had a pain, an agony, at the back of his eyes, but whether it was a racial appanage or something acquired, the *douceur* left him by a succession of girls, Atwater could not make up his mind. Atwater talked to various people he knew as he edged through the crowd towards Susan. When he arrived at where she was standing Verelst said:

"We always seem to be meeting."

"Yes, we do."

"How did your friend Pringle's show go?"

"Rather well."

Verelst said: "Susan is coming to see some pictures I bought the other day. I'd be so glad if you'd come as well."

Susan said: "He's got some superb drawings. I saw a few of them yesterday. You must come."

"Of course, I'd love to."

Verelst said: "I'm going to try and mix a drink for myself this time, Susan."

He moved off towards the bottles. Susan said: "Sit down here and talk to me."

Atwater said: "Will you dine with me after this?"

"I can't."

"When am I going to see you again?"

"I don't know."

"Why not?"

"I'm going away for a bit."

"For long?"

"No," she said. "Not for long."

"I never see you."

"I know," she said. "We must see more of each other when I come back."

"When are you coming back?"

"I don't know. Quite soon."

"I must see you before you go. Can't I see you before you go? I'm going away myself soon. We shan't meet again for ages."

She said: "What's the good of our going out together?"

"Well, I like it."

"But I'm not in love with you. I tell you I hate being in love. I don't want to be in love."

She began shaking the cocktail mixer, which she still held in her hand. She emptied the dregs, mostly orange-pips, into his glass and said:

"If you really want me to, I'll come out with you before I go."

"Of course I want you to."

"All right, I will. But I'm not going to fall in love with you."

"All right."

"I'm going away soon, so it wouldn't be very convenient."

She looked at him now with her big eyes. Atwater said:

"I'm sorry you're going away."

"I expect I'll be back soon. But I want to go." She said: "And now we must all have more, lots more, to drink."

The party was a great success and went on late. Susan herself disappeared, but whether or not with Verelst, Atwater was uncertain. He was hardly conscious that the party had ended until he found that he was alone in the room with Fotheringham and Mr Nunnery. Mr Nunnery said to Atwater:

"We've met before. I can't remember where."

"It was rather late one night. Weeks ago. We met at the top of your stairs. Susan had been dining with me."

"Of course," said Mr Nunnery. "Of course. I can't tell you what a good party I'd been to myself that night."

Fotheringham, who had been talking with great energy all the evening, now prowled round the room looking for a clean glass. Mr Nunnery said:

"Susan often goes out with you, doesn't she?"

Atwater said: "She's very hard to get hold of."

"I know, I know," said Mr Nunnery. "I never see her

at all myself. She tells me she's going away. Do I know where? Not a bit of it. I suppose you don't know?"

"I'm afraid I don't."

"I didn't expect you would," said Mr Nunnery. "And of course it's no business of mine, but I thought I'd just ask you in case you did."

"I don't a bit."

"Mere curiosity on my part."

Fotheringham had gone down on his hands and knees and was crawling slowly along the length of the sofa, to find out if any clean glasses had been put under it accidentally. He got up very suddenly and said:

"William, William, where are the clean glasses? I must have a clean glass."

"Why?"

"Germs. You can't be too careful."

Mr Nunnery said: "We might see if there is any food here and, if there is, eat it. I hope you will both stay."

"Can you put up with me?" said Fotheringham.

"I think we can."

"You're sure?"

"We're sure."

"Really?"

"Yes."

"If you're sure you can put up with me, I'll stay. And if there is a clean glass."

Mr Nunnery found some cheese and some sardines.

## 18

Mrs Race said: "But would it be wise? Would it be a good thing to do?"

Atwater said: "I don't know whether it would be either of those. It might be convenient."

"How long has he had it?"

"He's only just taken it. He heard about it from Undershaft, who used to live near there."

Mrs Race said: "Staying with Undershaft in the country would be one thing. Staying with Pringle would be another."

Atwater said: "There would be risks in both cases. Anyway, I've been asked because Apfelbaum, the picture man, has fallen through. Raymond told me so. I therefore go on the same terms."

"What terms?"

"Expediency."

"Will it be comfortable?"

"No."

Mrs Race said: "I can't make up my mind."

Atwater said: "It's very lucky that Dr Apfelbaum can't come. Staying in the same house, Raymond would be bound to be so rude to him that he'd make an enemy for life. As it is he may be of some use to Raymond one of these days."

Mrs Race said: "It's terrible what a little kindness may do. You remember that woman Jennifer?"

"Yes."

"Wauchop went to her head so much that she took to dropping in here two or three times a week at cocktail time."

"What did you do?"

"I have to get my typing done somewhere else," said Mrs Race. "Another woman, who's not nearly so cheap."

## 19

"Do you think it would amuse you?" said Atwater.

Susan said: "I think it might."

"Shall we go, then?"

"Yes. Let's go."

"And eat something after?"

"We might do that."

Atwater said: "We'd better go soon. It's the other side of the river."

They arrived there towards eight o'clock and found a small crowd outside waiting to get seats. They went to the left and up the stairs to the gallery. Susan said:

"I've never seen boxing before."

"It's amusing here. Better than one of the big fights."

The other side of the hall, where the unreserved seats were, was very full. Most of the reserved seats were filled as well, but there was no one sitting in the two seats next to Susan in the front row next to the gangway. There was another woman sitting in the row behind and several more down below in the seats round the ring. One of them was pretty and had a beige hat. The woman in the row behind them was not pretty. She was with a smallish man with a white mustache, who had a large imitation pearl in his tie and who said:

"They say at the door that it'll be a good night tonight."

The lights above the ring itself were enclosed in a large black square shade with advertisements for a newspaper printed round it in white and there were posters hung round the ropes of the ring advertising the program for next week and printed in red and blue. Referring to these the woman behind said:

"Will they take them down when they start?"

"Don't you worry," said the man.

The hall had a domed roof with pillars set at intervals round the gallery. The pillars were painted the color of chocolate and were theatrical in manner, like the permanent stage setting of a repertory company. They had well-designed cornices and the general effect was good. The domed roof was light yellow and the tobacco smoke came up from below and hung about it. Atwater bought a program. There were to be five fights during the evening. He said to Susan:

"The first two are called Young Moss and Jack Evans. Moss comes from King's Cross."

"Where does the other come from?"

"It just says Wales."

"What will they be like?"

"They'll be boys."

A man in a white sweater began to take the posters off the ropes. It was getting full downstairs and very hot, although it was a cool night outside. Atwater said:

"Do you really feel like that about everything?"

"Yes."

"Why?"

"I don't know," she said. "I just do."

Young Moss began to climb into the ring. He had neat black hair. Jack Evans came down the gangway after him. They were both thin and had black overcoats on their shoulders. The MC began to shout out their names and the bell went. There was nothing much between them in the first two rounds and they had just jumped about, hitting each other a good deal and not minding. Susan said:

"The Jew's really the better looking. But I like the other one best."

"He's the better boxer."

In the third round Evans went down for a rather lucky one from Moss's right, but, resting for a count of five, got up and landed several sound body punches one after another.

Neither of them took much trouble about keeping up a guard and they were both hitting hard. When the bell went Evans was pink in the face, but Moss's hair remained neat. Susan said

"How long do they go on for?"

"This one is only eight rounds."

"What will the others be?"

"Fifteen."

The MC did not take much notice of the fight and stood at one corner outside the ring by the gangway and talked to his friends. Moss and Evans were hard at it. Evans did well in the seventh round, but Moss won in the end. The boys shook hands and then kissed. Susan said:

"Did you see? They kissed."

"They often do that."

"Isn't that nice?"

Moss and Evans climbed out of the ring and went up the gangway towards the changing rooms. Atwater said:

"Do you dislike me, then?"

"Don't be silly."

"Why not?"

"Don't go on about it."

"I won't."

The next pair were also boys, but they were not so young as the first two and they were heavier. Neither of them was a very individual boxer, but, like the others, they both hit hard without keeping up much of a guard. They became inclined to clinch after the sixth round and the crowd got bored and shouted a bit, so they broke away, both of them rather puffed as the fight went on. The man behind with the imitation pearl in his tie said:

"Come on, boys. Come on."

"Did you see Carnera when he was over?" said the woman with him. The man said:

"Carnera?" in a way that meant that it was a silly question to have asked, but whether because he had seen him, or because he had not, it was impossible to say. The fight finished and the boy from Canning Town beat the one from Hoxton. Atwater said:

"How do you like it?"

"It's nice."

"This one is going to be more important."

"What are they?"

"Welterweights."

One of them had red drawers and a brown dressing-gown and the other had green drawers with a design on them like the sacred pentagram. The one with the pentagram on his drawers did not have a dressing gown round his shoulders. He had a woman's long coat, also green, but a it different shade from his drawers. When the time came to take off, he kissed it before he began to fight. He also kissed another piece of stuff he had in his hand. It was a piece of material, or garment. The second took it with the green coat when the bell went. Susan said:

"Why did he do that?"

Atwater said: "It's his girl's coat. He kissed it before he began to fight."

"Isn't that romantic?"

"Isn't it?"

"And what was the other thing?"

"I believe it's called a brassière, isn't it?"

"Was it that?"

"Yes."

"Is that his girl's too?"

"I don't know. Perhaps he's got two girls and one wears the coat and the other wears the whatnot."

"I think it's sweet."

"His having two girls?"

"I think it's sweet his kissing the things like that."

"Would you like me more if I did that sort of thing?"

"I like you all right," she said "What I tell you is that it is no good either of us liking the other."

"Why not?"

"It just isn't."

"Perhaps you're right."

"Of course I'm right." She said: "The man with the funny picture on his pants is a Jew, isn't he?"

"I expect so."

"What's his name?"

"Ernie Hyams. He comes from Bermondsey."

"I like Jews."

"I'd noticed it."

"They all behave like that," she said. "Kissing the coat, and so on."

"I know."

She laughed.

"How do you know?" she said.

"Anyway he's not going to win."

"Is that his girl sitting down there?"

"Probably."

The other man, the one who was wearing the red drawers and who looked like a boxer from an eighteenth-century caricature, because he had a low forehead and his nose spread all over his face, and pronounced muscles like an anatomical drawing, had the upper hand. He was called Gunner Haskins and he had a longer reach than the Jew, although Hyams was lighter on his feet and kept out of the way. Haskins was a bit careless where he hit. Halfway through the tenth round Hyams dropped his hands towards his left thigh and the whistle went. There were some boos. The woman behind said:

"He's all right. He wasn't hurt."

The man with her said: "And how do you know?"

"He's like Susan Lenglen," she said; "he doesn't want to be beaten."

"Don't you believe it," said the man with the imitation pearl pin. "Haskins hit him downstairs once before."

"He never."

"He did," said the man. "He's a good fighter, but he don't always look where he's hitting."

"He's a clean fighter."

"Well, he hit him downstairs that time," said the man. "On your sweet life."

The crowd booed a bit and someone shouted: "Why not kick him on the backside and have done with it?"

The seconds and the referee and the MC stood round Hyams. The crowd still booed at intervals. Haskins went back to his corner. Then he got up and went over to Hyams's corner. He spoke to Hyams and then put both his arms in the air and half lowered his head and waggled his gloves at the crowd to show that he knew he had gone wrong. Some of the crowd laughed and one or two clapped. The fight went to Hyams. There was an interval. Susan said:

"Anyway, if you feel like that, what about your little friend who wears the funny clothes?"

"What about her?

"Do you still see her?"

"Sometimes."

"Oh, God," she said. "I don't really care."

"I know you don't."

"I mean I understand all that."

"Yes?"

"Yes," she said. "That's not why."

"Why, then?"

"I don't know. Just I feel like that, I suppose."

"Yes, I see."

She said: "You're rather sweet really."

"Aren't I?"

"Yes. "But that's how I feel."

"Anyway, I never see you, so it doesn't make any difference."

"Well, if it doesn't make any difference?"

"Exactly."

"Don't be like that," she said.

"Why not?"

"I don't like it."

"Nonsense."

"No," she said. "I don't."

"It can't be helped. I am like that."

"You're being such a bore."

She said: "Why not be nice? You're so nice some times."

"I don't feel nice today."

The interval ended. The MC announced that there would now be a three-round trial. Susan said:

"Who are these?"

Atwater said: "A couple who haven't fought here before. They may be in some other job and thinking of becoming boxers or they may just be a couple who feel they'd like a fight. Did you hear their names?"

"No."

The trial pair were both big men. One of them had evidently been a sailor. The other might have been anything. He was tough-looking, but not at all like a professional boxer. He had hair growing outwards from the center of his head, like a Japanese doll. The bell went. The two moved towards each other and began hitting. Compared to these the boys in the earlier rounds had been cautious boxers. These two stood close up, hitting each other as hard as they could in the face without making any effort to keep up a guard. Sometimes they used their right, sometimes their left, but it was always to hit. The sailor had his left eye closed up early on. The crowd cheered first and then began to laugh. Susan said:

"All this blood is rather much, isn't it?"

"It's only a little really. They get it on their gloves and then all over them.

"I don't like the blood."

"It's only three rounds."

The first round was over. The man who was not the sailor went down once, but as soon as he was up again the bell went. There was a long pause.

"What's happened?"

"Goodness knows."

Someone arrived with another pair of drawers for the man who was not the sailor. He had split the ones he was wearing when he had gone down at the end of the first round. He slipped the new ones on over his old ones and the fight began again. They went on in the same way, getting close together and hitting hard. Then the man with hair like a Japanese doll and the two pairs of drawers hit the sailor a jab in the middle of the face, almost gently. The sailor went down heavily and slowly, like pushing over a sack of coals. He lay on the ground and did not get up. He was counted out and they came and carried him off the floor. There was a lot of cheering and some laughter. Someone threw a sixpence into the ring and the MC went inside the ropes and picked it up. Then more people threw some pennies until there was a good deal of money lying about. The MC picked them all up.

"Is that for them?"

"Yes."

"Why?"

"It's money."

After the trial rounds it was a Welshman again, thick and black-looking, and a tall, intellectual-faced man from Battersea. They fought differently from the boys and moved about on their feet and kept out of the way of each other's punches. It was not so amusing to watch because, although they were more scientific than the boys, neither of them boxed well. The crowd began to get bored again and shouted occasionally. The Welshman fought keeping his left leg very straight and sometimes making a curious stamping movement with it. Once in the sixth round he landed one with his left but it did not get home, although he jolted the other man against the ropes. They went on like this until the twelfth round. Then they both tried to buck up a bit, but by that time each had taken it out of the other too much for anything to happen. The Welshman had a trick of going back hard against the ropes and then coming off them with the additional impetus that they gave him when they pulled taut again, but even so he could not bring anything off. In the end the fair man with the intellectual expression won on points. A boy came down the gangway selling fruit. He said:

"Nice apples, two-pence. Nice apples."

Atwater said: "Have an apple?"

"No, you have one."

"I will."

Atwater gave the boy twopence and began to bite the apple. It was green and tasted of absolutely nothing. It was like eating material in the abstract. Susan said:

"I mean you know it couldn't be what's known as a success."

"Do I?"

"Of course you do."

"You're so lovely," he said. He dropped the core of the apple under the seat. He said:

"Anyway, I shall see you when you come back."

"Yes," she said, "Whenever that is."

"But you said it would be soon?"

"It will be soon. I don't know why I said that."

"Do you mean you're going away for ages?"

"No. Only a little time."

"We shall meet when you come back, shan't we?"

"I don't know. It always seems rather a business. Our meetings."

"Perhaps we'd better not, then?"

"I think we'd better not."

"You won't be away long, will you?"

"No," she said. "Not long."

The MC went into the ring before the last fight and announced that he was sorry to have to tell everyone that Jo Connor would not be able to fight that night as he had sprained his wrist. Instead, two others of the same weight would fight.

The MC was hoarse, so that it was not possible to hear what the names of the substitute couple were. The man behind said:

"The best bloody fight of the evening and we're not going to see it."

The woman with him said it was a shame for them to do such a thing. Somebody in the crowd shouted:

"What do you think we came here for?"

The MC repeated the names of the opponents loudly, and with great contempt for what the crowd thought. Again it was not possible to hear what the names were. Then the MC climbed out of the ring and went on talking to his friends by the gangway. There was a long pause, and then the last fight began. They were a nondescript couple whom the habitués of the place evidently knew pretty well. Neither of them was particularly young. They did not box badly, but there was nothing interesting about their fight. Atwater said:

"When do you go away?"

"I don't know exactly. Quite soon."

"Then I shall see you again in about a month? I'm going away for a bit myself."

"Yes. In about a month, I expect."

"This couple aren't very amusing, are they?"

"They're both so ugly."

"Aren't they?"

"They're a pair of bores."

Atwater said: "Perhaps you'll feel different when you come back."

"For goodness' sake."

"Sorry."

"Anyway, we're not going to meet."

"I forgot that."

The fight ended at last. Everyone got up and made for the gangways. Atwater and Susan waited until some of the crowd had cleared away before they tried to go down the stairs. Half-way down the stairs someone said:

"Well, I must say!"

Susan said: "Why, fancy meeting you here, Walter."

Walter Briskets who was with a very pale young man, said:

"Not at all. I made the place fashionable."

"Did you, Walter?"

"Of course I did."

Seeing there was no escape, Atwater said: "Are we all going in the same taxi?"

In this meridian of London summer it was melancholy, though not unpleasant, to sit and look out of the open window. Inside, the Middle West tramped and retramped the museum's corridors. Nosworth, questioning the man who had come to repair the waiting room chair, said:

"But why not until Tuesday?"

"We don't reckon to do it until then."

"Is there any reason for the delay?"

"We don't reckon to."

The man went away. Nosworth said to Atwater: "You go next week, don't you?"

"Yes."

"Abroad?"

"Home for a short time. Then I'm staying with Raymond Pringle in the country."

"The man who had the show?"

"Yes."

"Was it a success?"

"Quite."

Nosworth said: "I find this hot weather very exhausting."

When the window was wide open the smuts came into the room even more than usual and they lay thickly all over Atwater's desk and his papers. Atwater sat and wondered what had happened to Susan and whether it was somewhere far away where she was lying in the sun. He hoped that Dr Crutch would wait for the cooler weather before his next visit. The heat made the papers on the desk curl into spiral shapes and blisters came out on the walls' buff distemper.

# PART III—PALINDROME

Atwater looked about the platform, but Pringle had not yet arrived. There was one very old porter, deaf and partly mad, who had never heard of Pringle nor his house, so Atwater sat on a seat and waited. This was in fact the inevitable course to follow, as there were no trains to go back in, and walking was the only way that the porter could suggest of getting to the house. Atwater decided not to carry his suitcase across the downs and he sat on the seat and smoked. The porter rolled milk cans slowly from one end of the platform to the other. Then he rolled them back again. Atwater said: "It's a lovely day," but the porter would not answer.

It was about three quarters of an hour before Pringle appeared. When he came he was wearing khaki shorts and a yellow shirt open at the neck, his red hair making curious discords with his shirt and skin. He had not had his hair cut for several weeks.

"I couldn't get the car to start," he said. "Put your suitcase in the back. Mind that parcel. It's eggs. We don't want to have nothing to eat tomorrow."

Atwater got into the car.

"How far is it?"

"About five miles."

They drove along roads with downs on either side. There were wire fences and telegraph poles along the roads and the grass beside them was covered with a white dust. The dust rose in the air as they passed and hung in a cloud over the gorse and on one of the downs in the distance was a pumping station with domes and towers.

"How is everybody?" said Atwater. He was curious now who was staying with Pringle. Pringle said:

"Much as usual. We had rather a party last night."

"Did you?"

Pringle said: "God! I thought we weren't going to get up that last hill. This car will have to be overhauled."

There were not many cottages along the road. The wire stopped suddenly as the car reached some trees and they turned a corner in a cloud of dust and drove down a short grass lane.

"This is it," said Pringle.

It was an ugly little gray house standing in a hollow. There was no garden in front, but some outhouses made a sort of courtyard. Pringle stopped the car at the side of the house. There appeared to be no main entrance.

"Take your bag out," he said. "I'll put the car away and be back in a minute."

"Where are the others?"

"Hector and Sophy have gone for a walk. I believe Harriet is lying down upstairs."

"Harriet Twining?"

"Yes, of course."

Atwater went inside the house. He left his suitcase in the passage, where some mackintoshes were hung on the wall, and walked through the door at the end. A girl was clearing the table by easy stages. While she cleared she hummed in a rather high whine, *I wonder where my sweetie's hiding.* She had dark hair and looked anemic and the shape of her eyebrows made her seem as if surprised by sudden insult.

"Another hot day," said Atwater.

"That's right," said the girl.

He watched her tidying up. The room was in a mess and smelled of food and turpentine. Glasses with dregs in them were all over the place and someone had left a pair of trousers hanging over the piano. Atwater read a copy of *Vogue* that he found lying on the floor. After a while Pringle came in from putting the car away. He stood looking at the remains of lunch and the two empty bottles of Italian vermouth standing on the bookcase.

"I don't know what has happened to the car," he said. "It's all anyhow today." He sat down on a chair. Atwater said:

"Who have you got staying here?"

Pringle said: "Only Hector and Sophy and Harriet. Naomi Race may be coming later on." He said to the girl: "I've put the eggs in the kitchen. There's some Vim and soda too, so that you can take those canvases out of the bath and give it a wipe round. And by the way, the man put a new washer on the sink tap. It's working again now."

"Is that so?" said the girl.

"Yes," said Pringle. "It is." He said: "Come along, William. I'll show you your room."

They went upstairs.

"That is Miss Chalk," said Pringle. "She is called Ethel and Rod la Rocque is her favorite movie actor. I tell you that to prevent disappointment. You're frankly not her type. She doesn't much care for any of us. Would you like to wash?"

"Yes."

"There's no hot water."

"Then I won't wash."

"We none of us wash much here," said Pringle. "Let's go downstairs and have a drink. Then you can see some of the things I've painted."

Atwater put his suitcase down on the bed. It was a small whitewashed room with a tin washstand. Atwater said:

"I'll put some flannel trousers on."

He opened his suitcase. Pringle leaned against the post of the door.

"Don't be long," he said.

Someone came out of a room farther down the passage and slammed the door and came down the passage. It was Harriet. She stood in the open doorway of Atwater's room, rubbing her eyes and looking rather blowsy. Pretty but blowsy.

"Hullo, William," she said. "Why are you undressing at this time of day?" She held out her hand. Atwater pulled on his flannel trousers.

"How are you, Harriet?" he said.

"How's your headache, Harriet?" said Pringle.

"Like hell."

"Not better?"

"No," she said. "Like hell."

"Let's go and have a drink," said Pringle.

They went downstairs again to the dining room. Pringle began to shake up a cocktail. He shouted:

"Ethel, bring back some of those glasses when you've washed them."

The table had been cleared but the trousers remained draped over the piano as if in place of a Paisley shawl. The vermouth bottles were still on the bookcase.

"Let's go into the other room," said Harriet. "I like my conversation to have a background."

They went across the passage to another room which had French windows looking out on to the garden. There was a divan in it and a sofa and a table. One or two of Pringle's pictures hung on the walls. Harriet turned on the wireless and wound up the gramophone.

"How's London?" said Pringle.

Atwater said: "Pretty empty."

"No parties?"

"No. No parties."

"Any scandal?"

"I haven't heard any."

"What's happened to Susan?" said Harriet.

"She's been away. I haven't seen her for some time."

"You see a good deal of her as a rule, don't you?" said Pringle.

"I see her sometimes."

"She's so lovely," said Harriet.

Pringle said: "Who is this man Verelst who is always about with her now?"

Atwater said: "I introduced you to him at your private view."

"I know. But who is he?"

"He's just a man."

Harriet said: "I've met him. He's a Jew and not bad at all."

They watched Barlow and Sophy walking across the lawn. Barlow was still wearing his curiously small hat and thick suit. They came through the French windows, both very sunburnt. Pringle said:

"I wish you wouldn't leave your trousers in the dining room."

"Sorry," said Barlow. "Put them upstairs, Sophy. How are you, William?"

It was not easy to hear what anyone said, as the loudspeaker and the gramophone together made a lot of noise.

"How are you, William?" said Sophy, with just the same voice as Barlow, which she could do sometimes.

"For goodness' sake turn one of those off," said Pringle. "Preferably the talk on wild flowers. If you're really too keen on botany to forgo that, take that cursed *Bolero* off the gramophone."

His nerves did not seem to be in too good a state. He said:

"I'm going to have another look at the car."

Harriet sat down on the sofa and began to read Vogue. Sophy went upstairs with the trousers. Barlow said to Atwater:

"Come and see the garden."

Atwater followed him on to the lawn, which was marked out for tennis. There were trees on the far side and fields beyond. They walked towards the trees. Atwater said:

"What's Harriet doing here?"

"She got fed up with Gosling. Or he got fed up with her. So she came here."

"To Raymond?"

"Yes."

"How long has she been here?"

"About a week. She's getting bored."

"Is she?"

"She's a funny girl."

"How do you mean, funny?"

Barlow said: "Oh, just funny. You never know what she will do next." He laughed. "I shouldn't think Raymond will keep her long," he said.

"Sophy looks very well."

"She's all right. She and Harriet get on very well together."

"Do they?"

"You'd never think they would."

They went as far as the trees, where there was some wire and a ditch that stopped them going farther. Fields began on the other side of the ditch. They turned towards the house again. There were a few clouds coming up over the downs from behind the pumping station, which was a long way off but could be seen from the garden through the trees. When they came back into the sitting-room the gramophone was still playing and Harriet was sitting by herself smoking a cigarette. Barlow went upstairs and left Atwater alone with her.

"Where have you been?" she said.

Atwater said: "To the end of the garden." He said: "I didn't know that you knew Raymond."

"I've known him for ages."

"Now I remember introducing you."

Harriet said: "At the moment I'm his mistress, if that sets your curiosity at rest at all."

"Really?"

"Yes."

"That always sounds such a pompous thing to be."

"Of course, it is rather."

"What does one do here?" he said.

"Nothing."

"Rather pleasant."

"Lovely."

"It seems nice air and so on."

"It is."

"After London."

"Yes," she said. "After London."

Atwater said: "I hear we don't wash here."

"There's bathing." She stopped talking to him and picked up a book.

Atwater went up to his room and unpacked his bag.

## 22

After he had brushed his hair, Atwater lay on his bed and wondered where Susan was and if he would ever see her again. After he had wondered about this for a short time he got up and brushed his hair again and went downstairs. The others were in the sitting room. Pringle said:

"I don't know what's wrong with the car. It won't go at all now."

"How are you going to amuse your guests this evening, Raymond?" said Harriet.

Pringle said: "I thought we might all go round to the local pub. It's called the Goat, if that adds to its attractions for anybody."

Ethel came in to say that dinner was ready. She gave them all a withering look. Pringle said:

"We are rather short of plates. We broke some last night, but I expect we can manage."

Atwater said: "What happened last night?"

"Oh, nothing," said Pringle. "We broke a few things. I don't know what Ethel thought about it."

"She's got a very cynical look, that girl," said Harriet.

Barlow said: "She doesn't care."

"Not she," said Sophy.

"You've had to get used to some things too, Sophy," said Pringle. Sophy smiled at him. She had a slow, wide smile that made her mouth seem bigger than it really was. She did not mind being teased about the days when Barlow had first found her and taken her away from the secretary of a suburban golf club and taught her about things.

They ate. It was a good dinner of its kind and there was some drinkable claret. Both the girls drank gin-and-ginger-ale.

After dinner, Pringle said:

"We might make some coffee in the machine."

Harriet said: "No. For heaven's sake not. It takes all night. Let's go to the pub or it will be shut before we get there."

"Don't forget your medicine, Raymond," said Sophy. She always remembered that sort of thing. Pringle said:

"I nearly did." He began to pour it out. "Thank you, Sophy," he said. Sophy smiled again. Harriet said:

"Take it with you. Or we'll start without you. One or the other."

Pringle drank some out of the bottle. He made a face.

"I'm ready now," he said. Sophy went upstairs to get a coat, as it was cool. The moon was behind clouds, so that it was dark outside. They went up the lane. Pringle said it was about twenty minutes to the village. As they turned into the main road he took Harriet's arm. Atwater walked with Sophy, and Barlow, in his small hat, went a little way ahead of the rest of them, hunched up with his hands in his pockets.

"What does the village consist of?" said Atwater.

"Two pubs and a church. But we can't go into one of

the pubs because Undershaft bit the potman when he stayed here last summer."

"That's not like him."

"He's got quite a weak head," said Pringle. "The Goat is much better than the Lord Nelson, so it didn't really matter."

"Did he stay here long?"

"He had a cottage in the village last summer and the summer before. It was through him I heard of my place."

"I suppose most of the people in the village are journalists and so on."

"Most of them are, of course. But then they go to the Lord Nelson, so one doesn't see them. But that's why we don't go into the village much. And of course that was what upset Undershaft that night."

"The neighbors?"

"Of course."

They passed two or three cottages and the church. The Goat stood a little way back from the road and had a strip of grass in front of it. Pringle pushed the door open and Harriet and Sophy went in first. The bar was large and fairly crowded. Darts and shove-half penny were being played.

"'Arlots," said a voice from the other end of the bar as they sat down.

"Oh no, we're not," said Harriet. "We're nothing of the sort, so just you keep quiet."

The barman was embarrassed. He wore a cap and gaiters and had a small close-clipped mustache. He went red. Pringle ordered a round of drinks, and said:

"Great weather for the harvest."

"That's right," said the barman.

They watched two young men in purple suits and gamboge pointed shoes playing shove-half penny. Harriet spilt some of her drink on the board.

"So sorry," she said, and smiled at the players, who looked angry. One of them wiped the drink off with a bandana handkerchief and they went on with the game. Pringle leant at the bar. He said:

"Is Cheadle far from here?"

The barman said: "Couldn't say. I'm a stranger in these parts."

Implying the climax of not a few generations of squirearchy in the neighborhood, Pringle said:

"I have a house here."

"Oh yeah," said the barman, on the spot but not greatly intrigued. He whistled and jogged sideways, a little behind the bar, doing a sort of bastard Charleston. Pringle leant there and sipped his drink. The two young men finished their game of shove-half penny. They stood back and lit cigarettes.

"Come on," said Pringle. "I'll take you on, Hector."

He said it with a rather terrifying burst of nervous heartiness and, leaving his drink at the bar, he came over to the board. Barlow picked up the duster and wiped off the chalk of the last game. Harriet said:

"No. Hector and I will take on you and William. Sophy can umpire.

"I'll umpire," said Sophy.

Atwater started off and placed two. The game was

pretty level. Barlow and Pringle played about equally. Atwater always put in at least one. Harriet often sent them all up to the end of the board, but more than once fluked five.

The lower beds were filled up early, but the game went slowly after this and the third chalk in Annie's bed was elusive. Barlow sent his fifth up with a neat tap. It sailed into London.

"At last," he said.

"It's tight," said Pringle.

Barlow leaned across the board and stared for some time at the ten-centime piece.

"No," he said, "it's not tight as far as I can see."

He looked round for Harriet, who as it was not her turn had left the table and was throwing darts into the target, while the two yellow-shod young men who had been playing shove-half penny gloomily watched her. Barlow turned to Atwater.

"What do you think?" he said.

Atwater said: "I don't think it's actually on the line. It's difficult to see in this light."

"What do you think, Sophy?" said Barlow. "You're umpire."

Sophy said: "Well, I don't know the rules properly about that."

Barlow said: "It's not a question of knowing the rules. It's a question of eyesight. Can you see space or can't you?"

"Well, I don't know," she said

Barlow said: "You're half-baked."

193

Pringle said: "It doesn't make any difference. The way they play it down here is that it's tight if there's any doubt about it."

Atwater said: "Is this the sort of board where the brass lines lift up?"

It was. Atwater lifted up the line from the side of the board. It did not touch the half penny. Pringle said:

"That doesn't matter. The way they play the game in this part of the world is that it's tight if there's any question about it."

"Why have the lines so that they lift up, then?"

"I don't know."

"It seems a funny way to play it."

"It may be, but there it is."

"I suppose I shall have to take your word for it."

"Ask any of the people here."

"I shan't," said Barlow. "I don't like speaking to strangers. You never know how they'll take it."

Harriet came back from the target. She said:

"Is it my turn again yet?"

She had a dart in her hand. She said:

"I seem to have done something to the point of this. It missed the target and fell on the floor."

Sophy took the dart in her hands.

"Why, you've broken the top off," she said.

"That's it," said Harriet.

"We've lost the game, Harriet," said Barlow.

"Oh, Hector. What an ass you are."

Barlow said: "Yes, it was all my fault, wasn't it?"

"Yes," she said. "You're an ass."

In the other bar some villagers began to sing in a dispirited way on three notes: "*Oh, show me the way to go home, for I'm tired and I want to go to bed…*"

"One more round before we go," said Barlow.

"Now then, ladies and gentlemen," said the barman. "Time, please."

Sophy refused a last drink. The others had beer.

"Drink up, ladies and gentlemen," said the barman.

Pringle said: "There must be five minutes yet. Don't hurry."

"There's not," said Atwater. "It's just on time. This is the country."

The barman came the other side of the counter.

"Time, please," he said.

Harriet said: "You mustn't hurry a lady drinking a pint of beer. The effects might be fatal."

The barman was not amused. He took Harriet's glass from her. Pringle, Barlow and Atwater gulped down their pints.

"Take it," said Harriet. "Take it. But for goodness' sake take my advice as well and don't drink it. I wouldn't wash my car down with the stuff."

"We're closing now," said the barman. None of them amused him at all. He put all the glasses one inside the other and took them behind the bar. Then he held the door open for them to go out.

"Good night," said Pringle.

"So long," said the barman.

They went out on to the strip of grass in front of the Goat. It was bright moonlight outside. The people who had been in the pub were standing about in groups, having the last word and settling points with regard to local morals. As they came out, two persons left one of the large groups and moved toward them. They were an elderly couple, a man and a woman. They went toward Pringle, and the man said:

"What I says is, Mr Pringle: that it can't go on, because it's the same day in day out and our Ethel's a respectable girl, and what with not at home till eleven o'clock one night and goings on—it isn't the same as London, Mr Pringle; in a little place folks talk and what one says the other repeats and we've got to look after our girl."

"Who are you?" said Pringle. He had been forced to drink his last pint of beer hurriedly and was not at once prepared to enter into so heated a discussion. He swallowed painfully. Then he recovered himself and began twitching. The woman said:

"It's like this, Mr Pringle, last Sunday I saw my sister-in-law smiling to herself, and I asked her: 'What are you laughing at, Hazel,' I said. 'Thoughts,' she said, and she said: 'There's a girl in the paper here that ran away from home after seeing goings on at the pictures,' she said. 'That's what your Ethel will be doing one of these days,' she said."

"What's all this?" said Harriet.

"Ethel's parents think you're a bad influence on her," said Pringle. "All right, take the girl away if you want to."

"Nonsense," said Harriet. "We can't be without a maid. Offer her higher wages, Raymond."

"Excuse me, miss," said Mr Chalk. "It not being a matter of wages. Ethel gets a fair wage."

Harriet went closer to him. She took his arm and said:

"No, of course it isn't, Mr Chalk. I know just how you feel about it, and I should be just the same if she were my daughter. But it's hard work and Mr Pringle is going to pay Ethel another ten shillings a week."

"Right's right and wrong's wrong," said Mrs Chalk.

Pringle said: "Well, I don't promise."

"Now, Raymond," said Harriet, "Don't be so mean. Remember you are our host and how uncomfortable we are, anyway. You can easily afford another ten bob a week."

"Right's right and wrong's wrong," said Mrs Chalk, angry about the continued squeezing of her husband's arm by Harriet. Pringle said:

"Well, it would be very inconvenient for Ethel to go, so shall we say five shillings extra?"

"Raymond, you're so grasping," said Harriet.

"Five shillings?" said Pringle.

Mrs Chalk said: "You can't go making terms."

"Now, mother," said Mr Chalk.

"Well?" said Pringle.

The moon had come out from behind a bank of clouds and the moonlight was strong enough for Atwater to see Mr Chalk's face quite clearly. He was a bright-eyed little man. Atwater watched him wink. Mrs Chalk was obdurate.

"Right's right and wrong's wrong," she said. She gave Harriet a look.

"I hope that will be satisfactory," said Pringle.

"That's OK, Chief," Mr Chalk hazarded.

Harriet gave Mr Chalk's arm a last pat. Mr Chalk had his head rather on one side as they said good night to him.

They started back towards the house. Atwater looked over his shoulder when they had gone a little way and saw that Mrs Chalk was still talking to her husband.

## 23

Naomi Race arrived two or three days after Atwater. She brought a good deal of luggage with her and a dog. When Pringle showed her the room she was going to have she thought he was joking; but she stayed in the end because she had made no other plans. After a time she became accustomed to the place, only she insisted on having two more chairs in her bedroom, so Pringle took one from Atwater's room and one from the room that Barlow and Sophy were in. Mrs Race seemed happy after that, though she often grumbled about there being no hot water. Her dog got in the way and was not house-trained, but in the end everybody grew used to that as well.

Sometimes they played tennis. Mrs Race and Barlow played against Sophy and Pringle. Mrs Race used to say that she had learned tennis at school soon after it had superseded croquet as a fashionable sport and she served underhand screws that Pringle could not take. Sophy always looked at Barlow when he served instead of at the ball. She watched him with a curious cow-like approval as if she were in a trance, and she came back to life only after the stroke had been lost, so that in spite of Pringle's smashing cuts at the net the others won more often than not. Pringle did not much like losing. One of the reasons that he disliked it was because he knew that he could beat Barlow when they played singles. Besides, Mrs Race's service annoyed him. There was no netting round the court, and balls disappeared among the bushes.

"We started with two boxes of them," said Pringle. "And now there are only four."

He swore a good deal and very loud. Ethel watched disapprovingly from the scullery window, where she was doing the washing up. Harriet was her favorite of the whole party. She found none of the men up to standard.

"That was a line ball, wasn't it?" said Barlow.

"No," said Pringle. "It was out."

Harriet, playing with her manicure set as she lay on a rug beside the court, looked up.

"It wasn't. It was on the line," she said. "Don't try and cheat, Raymond."

"It was out," said Pringle.

"It was not," said Harriet.

Barlow said: "I think it was out, as a matter of fact. The sun was rather in my eyes."

They had the service again. There were two long rallies and two more balls went into the bushes, one from an animated underhand drive by Pringle and the other lobbed into the air, and a long way away, by Sophy. Mrs Race refused to continue the game unless there were at least three balls to play with. The set was therefore abandoned. Pringle wandered about among the laurels looking for balls and after a bit Sophy went to help him. Atwater marked the place in *Urn Burial* with a piece of silver paper from Harriet's box of cigarettes and followed Barlow into the house. As he came through the French window Barlow was in front of the easel on which Pringle's latest work stood. They both looked at it for some little time. Barlow said:

"Poor Raymond. No talent. He can't even write."

He examined the canvas intently.

"I often think of the masters at school," he said. "Men who could have made fortunes merely by walking across a music hall stage preferred to teach little boys mathematics."

"No doubt they had their reasons."

"No doubt."

Harriet came in from the garden dragging the rug along the ground behind her. She put her arms round their shoulders and looked at the picture with them. She said:

"You've got it the wrong way up."

Barlow put an arm under her knee and carried her to the sofa.

"What are we going to do?" he said.

Harriet said: "Why not all bathe?"

"Will you come and bathe, William?"

"Yes, I'll bathe."

Barlow went to the French window again. Pringle and Sophy were still looking for balls. Mrs Race was sitting in a deck chair fanning herself. Barlow shouted:

"Are you all coming to bathe?"

Mrs Race was the only one who heard what he had said, and she shouted back:

"Certainly not."

"Are you coming to bathe?" shouted Barlow again. Sophy and Pringle came towards him. They had found quite a lot of balls between them. Some of the balls were ones that had been lost two days before and had got rather wet. Pringle said:

"Are we what?"

"Coming to bathe?"

Sophy shook her head and smiled. Bathing was one of the things she did not like. Barlow had only once persuaded her to go into the sea, and then she had come out immediately and said that she did not like it at all. Since then she would never attempt it again, but she was quite happy going down to the beach and watching the rest of them bathe. Pringle said:

"No, I shan't. I don't feel like it."

Harriet said: "Raymond, you're not angry because I said you cheated at tennis, are you?"

"Of course I don't care what you say."

"I believe you are."

Pringle touched her head with his hand.

"No, I'm not," he said. He looked pleased that she had asked him if he were angry. Harriet said:

"Well, we're all going to bathe. Aren't you really coming?"

"No. I don't want to now."

He was no longer in a bad temper, but he did not want to bathe. He said:

"I'm going to put these balls in front of the kitchen

fire. They'll really be quite all right to play with when they've dried a bit."

He went into the house. Harriet said:

"I haven't made him in a bad temper for the rest of the day, have I?"

Barlow said: "He's all right. Go upstairs and get your bathing things. William's and mine are in the scullery."

"Isn't he perfect about things like tennis balls?" she said.

Atwater did not stay in the sea long because it was beginning to be cold as evening drew on. He came out and dried himself, and put on his trousers, while he watched Barlow and Harriet, who were in shallow water having an argument. Barlow had a long body and short strong legs. The salt water did not seem to have any effect on his stubbling black hair, which still looked as if he had not immersed his head at all, although he had been swimming about under the surface. In her bathing dress you noticed that Harriet was getting just a little too fat, thought Atwater. As he watched them Harriet gave Barlow a push with her hand that made him fall backwards into the sea. Then she turned away from him and swam into the deeper water. Barlow splashed the water out of his eyes and followed her. Atwater watched them and threw a few stones at the other parts of the sea. After that he finished his dressing and lay on his back on the shingle and waited for them. Barlow was the next to come in. He said:

"Hell. I've stayed in too long. I'm cold."

Harriet came in too after a few moments and they went back to the house.

The car was hopelessly out of order. Pringle kept on saying that he must get someone to come and have a look at it. One day he actually wrote a letter to a garage in the neighborhood. They went for walks and bathed and Barlow did a good deal of painting. Pringle's nerves were better than they had been for a long time. Harriet was amusing but restless. She still looked more blowsy than she had ever been in London.

Pringle had been in pretty good form all day. Barlow said:

"What's come over him? It's like when one of the critics said there was a quality of originality about his treatment of water."

"When he rang up Pauline de Chabran at Claridge's?" said Atwater.

"The week he told Mrs Beamish her parties were the worst in Europe."

"But he's never been to one."

"That was what made her so angry," said Barlow. He said: "Will you be going back with us on Monday?"

"To work?"

"Yes."

Barlow said: "I shall be sorry to go. I shall be sorry to see no more of Harriet, for one thing."

"She'll be in London soon."

"Yes, she'll be in London soon," said Barlow. "You know I've been thinking whether I ought to marry Sophy. Or do you think Miriam would be better? Julia, of course, you don't know."

Pringle came into the sitting room. He was smoking a cigar. He said:

"They need waking up, these village people. They don't understand modern methods."

"Who is it now?"

"The girl in the paper shop."

"The one with iron spectacles?"

"She said if I didn't like the papers being late why didn't I live elsewhere."

"She's not a bad-looking girl," said Barlow. "Of a type."

"Then there's the butcher," said Pringle. "But I woke them both up."

Barlow said: "It's curious, that girl in the paper shop. If you took her glasses off she wouldn't be bad at all."

Pringle was certainly in very good form. After dinner he suggested walking on the downs. Barlow had canvases to prepare, so he would not come. Sophy was feeling sick from eating too many peaches and went to bed early. Harriet said she was too idle and Mrs Race wanted to finish her book. So Atwater and Pringle went off together. They went through the village and turned up a sandy lane towards the downs. Pringle was very cheerful and said: "Nice evening" or "Rain going to hold off?" to all the people they met. Pringle said he thought he should live in the country always. It was a more natural life than living in some town. Besides, he wanted time to do a lot of painting. They climbed the hill until the sea was in sight. There were a few trees on the top of the hill and they sat under them and smoked, facing towards the sea. Pringle said:

"I shouldn't like to live with a girl like Sophy. I mean those peaches and so on. Even Hector felt that."

Atwater said: "I could never be more than a friend to any fat girl."

They watched a couple coming up the hill to their right. The girl had a red face and the man was wearing a check cap and blue serge suit with short tight trousers and very light socks. They reached the top of the hill and sat on a log on the other side of the clump of trees. The man put his arm round the girl's waist. He did not take his cap off. Pringle said:

"There's something universal about love."

"Certainly."

"Don't you think?"

"I do."

"Take that couple over there."

He took them and continued for some time. Atwater listened to quite a lot of what Pringle was saying and when it became out of the question to listen any more he thought about Susan and if he would be able to see her on Monday night or whether she would still be away. The sun glanced sharply off some of the pumping station's towers on a remote down. Pringle brought the more general part of his extempore reflections to an end and said:

"Now Harriet. What do you think about her?"

"How do you mean, what do I think about her?"

"Well, what do you think about her?"

"As a woman?"

"Do you think she would make a good wife?"

"It seems to depend on what you mean by good."

"You must know what I mean by good."

"On the contrary."

"But what do you think about marrying her?"

"I shan't do it."

"Of course, she'd be too civilized for Hector. He likes something more straightforward."

"Don't suggest it to him. He proposes to far too many women as it is."

"Don't joke," said Pringle. "Harriet and I are probably going to get married."

"Really?"

"Yes."

"Congratulations."

"Thanks," said Pringle. "We like each other a good deal."

Atwater said: "That always makes marriage more satisfactory, if you both like each other a lot."

"We do."

"I'm delighted to hear it."

"I think she's lucky in a way."

The couple on the log sat in silence. They had moved closer together under the influence of the unrestrained crimsons of the sunset. Atwater said: "I shall be sorry to go back on Monday."

"I'm glad there was room for you," said Pringle. "Though it was a great pity Dr Apfelbaum couldn't come, as Hector and I both wanted to talk to him about the picture market. However, it can't be helped."

"You may be able to get hold of him later."

"I doubt it."

Atwater said: "Shall we be getting back?"

They got up, and Pringle threw away the end of his cigarette. He said:

"I think she'll make a good wife."

The lovers had moved off the log and lay on the ground sideways, looking at each other's faces. The man still kept his cap on.

Pringle looked towards the sea. He said:

"You get a very special light on these downs in the early morning. I shall stay here for some time, I think, and do some painting." He said: "Then I shall have another small show in the spring."

Atwater and Pringle went back across the fields. It was dark now and sometimes it was difficult to find gaps in the hedges to climb through. Once Pringle put his foot into a rabbit hole and thought he had twisted his ankle, but even so he remained in a very good temper. In some of the hollows of the downs there was a hanging vapor, almost a mist. They arrived at the end of the garden and had to jump over the ditch and climb the wire. There was a flash of summer lightning as they went into the garden and in the shadows the house did not look so ugly. They walked over the flower beds toward the sitting room. Pringle pushed open the French windows and went in. Atwater came in behind him. The room was dark. Pringle said:

"Have you got a match?"

Atwater struck a match and went toward the mantelpiece where the oil lamp stood. Pringle said:

"Why on earth are you sitting in the dark?"

Atwater lighted the lamp and turned round toward the room. Barlow and Harriet were on the sofa. Both of them looked a bit disheveled and Pringle, who was never very quick about taking things in, said:

"Why are you sitting in the dark? It's a lovely evening outside."

He put the lamp on the table and turned it full on. Harriet began to put on her shoes. Her hair was rather untidy. She could not find one shoe.

"Look here, I say," said Pringle. It suddenly dawned on him.

"Where the hell is my shoe?" said Harriet. She knelt down and looked under the sofa.

"Look here, you know," said Pringle. He was angry now. Very angry. Atwater wondered what was going to happen. Harriet found the other shoe and began to put it on. She put her hands on her hips and wriggled more thoroughly into her dress. She said:

"Give me a cigarette, somebody."

Atwater gave her a cigarette and lighted it. He took one himself and looked at Barlow. Barlow's hair was standing up on end like Harriet's and this gave him a curiously surprised look, though it was less noticeable because of the curious roughness of its texture. Now it looked as if he wore it *en brosse*.

"I always suspected as much," said Pringle.

Barlow did not say anything, but he took his pipe from his pocket and began to fill it. There did not seem to be much to say. Harriet gave a touch to her hair. Then she yawned and said:

"Well, I'm going to bed now, boys and girls. I'm tired."

She filled her cigarette case and slammed the door behind her.

"You're a cad," said Pringle.

Barlow said: "What?"

"A cad," said Pringle. "A cad." Barlow did not take the word in at first. Then he said:

"I know. We both are. You said so only yesterday, when we were talking about Olga."

Pringle was quite breathless. He kept putting his hands in his pockets and taking them out again. Atwater had never seen him twitch so much. Barlow began to light his pipe.

"Look here," he said, "I'm very sorry about this."

"I've seen it coming for some time," said Pringle.

Barlow left off lighting his pipe and looked up. He said:

"Well, why the hell didn't you warn me? I was never so surprised in my life."

Pringle said: "You've been a bad influence on me ever since I met you. I've even felt my painting getting worse and worse."

"In what way?"

"In every way."

"I'm sure you're wrong."

"I know I'm right"

Barlow said: "How you put the paint on or the subjects you choose?"

Really interested, he had stopped lighting his pipe.

"I always disliked you," said Pringle. His voice had

become so high that he was nearly screaming. Barlow struck another match.

"I'm very sorry about this," he said.

"Sorry?" said Pringle. "Sorry?"

"Anyway, I'll leave tomorrow."

Somebody opened the door and came into the room. It was Mrs Race, with a long cigarette holder in her hand, wearing a curious green Chinese garment. She said:

"Must you all make this noise?"

Pringle said:

"Yes, we must make this noise. I go out of the house for two minutes and I come back and find this man on the sofa with the girl I'm engaged to. Curse the whole lot of you. I shall make as much noise as I choose." He said to Barlow:

"I'll drive you to the station tomorrow as early as you like."

"What trains are there tomorrow?" said Barlow.

Mrs Race said:

"There aren't any. It's Sunday. Anyway, you both know as well as I do that the car is out of order and will be until the garage man comes to see it. He promised to come on Sunday night. Whether he will or not is another matter."

"Monday, then," said Pringle.

"Monday," said Barlow.

Mrs Race said: "If I go back to bed, can I have any sort of guarantee that you will all of you make a little less noise?"

Pringle said: "No, you can't. It's my house, and I shall make as much noise as I like."

Mrs Race shrugged her shoulders. She said:

"You men have such bad tempers." She said "Good night" to Atwater and went upstairs again.

There was a pause. It was one of those situations when it did not make much difference whether you were in the right or in the wrong, if regarded purely from the point of view of development. That was how Atwater felt about it. Pringle said:

"I'm going to lock up the house."

He went out. They heard him locking doors and drawing bolts. Barlow said:

"I think I've put my foot in it."

"So do I," said Atwater.

"What do you think?"

"You're mad."

They heard Pringle upsetting pots and pans in the kitchen and cursing. There was a tremendous noise as he upset what must have been the dust bin. He turned off several levers and banged a window to. Barlow said:

"I've made a fool of myself."

Atwater said: "Yes, you have."

In the kitchen, Pringle cursed and rattled things about. Then he shouted:

"Here, I say."

"What?" said Atwater.

"Come here."

Atwater went into the kitchen. There was no one there, so he went on into the scullery. Pringle was in the scullery. He had caught his coat in the levers and handle where the water was turned off. He was standing on the sink and was twisted round at an angle. Atwater climbed up on to the sink and pulled. They both pulled and pulled. Pringle cursed.

"Don't tear the coat," he said.

"I'm not."

"You will if you go on pulling like that."

"No, I don't think I shall."

"Yes, you will."

It looked as if Pringle would have to be cut out of his clothes, or stand on the sink all night until it was possible to get hold of the plumber. Atwater was out of breath with pulling. Pringle remained fixed in among some odds and ends of taps and a small wheel. Atwater said:

"Shall I get Hector?"

Pringle cursed. They pulled again a good deal. Then Barlow came in to see what was wrong and why Pringle was making so much noise. He said:

"Can I help?"

Atwater said: "Yes."

Atwater and Barlow lifted Pringle bodily into the air to take the weight off his coat. By pulling again in this position they managed to get it free, but it took several minutes to do. Then they lit the candles that were on the scullery table and went to bed. Pringle was white in the face. No one said good night to anyone else.

Atwater went into his room. He closed the door.

He noticed that there were several large spiders on his pillow, and caught them one after another in his toothglass and dropped them out of the window, but did not interfere with the moths that had collected round the candle. In bed he lay awake for a short time, considering matters. Then he went to sleep.

## 27

That morning the atmosphere in the house was not good. Barlow went off to paint after an early breakfast. He had breakfasted so early that Atwater on his way to the bathroom had seen him already leaving the house with an easel under his arm. Atwater dressed and arrived downstairs at the same time as Sophy. No one else was there. Sophy said good morning and smiled. Atwater wondered how much Barlow had told her, but he thought that she was used to Barlow and Pringle having quarrels and he did not say anything about the night before. Sophy poured him out the coffee and said:

"So Barlow and Raymond have been at each other again."

She never in any circumstances called Barlow by his Christian name. Atwater said:

"Yes, they have."

"Aren't they silly?"

She seemed quite happy and had recovered from her surfeit of peaches. She sat there smiling to herself and after breakfast she took her work basket and began to mend some of Barlow's socks.

"Aren't they all late?" she said.

Then Harriet appeared. Harriet had made herself up a good deal and looked composed. She talked a lot and ate a large breakfast; but at the same time the atmosphere was not good. Mrs Race never arrived downstairs before lunch and there was no sign of Pringle. After breakfast Harriet did her nails and Sophy darned Barlow's socks. She did not do this very well and Barlow usually had to throw the socks away afterwards, as they were so lumpy, but the fact that she darned them at all gave them both a feeling of confidence in each other. Atwater read the copy of *Vogue,* including the advertisements for removing hair, as he now knew nearly all the rest of it by heart and it was too early in the morning to go on with *Urn Burial.*

Harriet said: "Let's go and sit on the cliffs. I don't like indoors today."

Sophy said she had promised to meet Barlow at the old sawmill at twelve, so that it would hardly be worth while her coming. Otherwise she said it would have been ever so nice to have gone on the cliffs.

"You must come with me, William," said Harriet.

Sophy sat darning socks for a bit before she went to meet Barlow at the old sawmill, because she knew that he would not like it if she arrived too early. Atwater and Harriet started out.

It was sunny and cool as they walked toward the sea. Harriet had no hat and no stockings, but she had made up her face very successfully. They walked a little way along the road and then climbed the wire that ran alongside of it and struck across the downs. The air was fresh, rather metallic and Scandinavian. After crossing several fields they found a place to lie in the sun from where they could see the beach below them in each direction. They lay on the grass watching the sea and there was a smell of seaweed that came up to them from the beach. They could see one or two boats. Harriet said:

"William, I'm so unhappy."

"Are you?"

"Things are always going wrong."

"Yes?"

"Have you a cigarette?"

He gave her a cigarette and watched her lying there smoking it. She had good legs, which were brown from the sun, and the sun had also bleached some of her hair, so that two or three curls of it were lighter than the rest. She looked at Atwater with her eyes half shut.

"Don't you think I've made rather a mess of things?"

"Yes, I think you have."

She laughed and rolled over on her front.

"Look," she said. "There's Raymond."

Atwater sat up and looked towards the beach. Pringle, wearing a suit, was walking along it slowly with his hands in his pockets and taking very long strides that made him seem smaller than he really was. Harriet said:

"Do you think it would be better if he grew a beard?"

They watched Pringle now instead of the sea. He went on until he was nearly underneath them, where they could see him but he could not see them. He stood there for a moment and then took off his wristwatch and put it in his pocket. He began to undress. As he stripped he folded up his clothes and made a neat pile of them.

"Raymond shouldn't undress like that in broad daylight on the most open part of the beach," said Harriet. "Anybody might come along. Absolutely anybody. Some people might not like it."

Atwater said: "He's forgotten his towel."

They watched Pringle undressing. At last he was naked. He stood there looking at the sea with his hands on his hips. He was white up to his neck, and his head was brown and large and made him look top-heavy. The sun made his hair very red.

"He's got a bad body," said Harriet.

Pringle stood there scratching himself. He did this for some time and then walked towards the sea. He stepped gingerly, as the stones evidently hurt the soles of his feet, and when he reached the sea he stopped and looked back in the direction of the house. Harriet said:

"He's just remembered his towel."

But Pringle went on into the water. He stepped high, as if he were marking time and splashed the water away from his ankles. The water suddenly became deeper. It came up to his waist and he dropped forward and began to swim. The sun caught his arm as he swam away from them, doing a pretentious side stroke. The sea looked very blue and there was mist on the horizon. They watched him for a short time. His head was like some curious red fruit floating along in the water. Then he swam into the sun and it was difficult to see him. Harriet got up and stretched herself. She said:

"Let's walk towards the woods."

"Why?"

"It's nice there."

"Is it?"

"Yes."

Atwater got up from the grass. He looked down at the sea, but Pringle's head was no longer in sight. The mist on the horizon was thickening. There were a number of small boats with sails moving along, and farther away a black boat with a funnel and smoke. They turned away from the cliffs and going through the hedge made their way across some ploughlands. There were deep furrows, so that they had to step from the top of one furrow to the top of another and take either too long or too short steps. Harriet stumbled and took his arm. She said:

"Are you in love with anybody, William?"

"Yes."

"Are you?"

"I've just said I am."

"So am I, but I never see him, so what's the good?"

"I don't know."

The plough ended, and they passed into woods where sun came slanting through the branches. In a clearing, a hollow with a bank on either side, Harriet sat down and Atwater sat beside her. She said:

"Do you think that one of these days everything will come right?"

"No."

"Neither do I," she said. She laughed again.

Atwater said: "What's going to happen about all this?"

"I don't know," she said, "yet."

"What do you think?"

"I don't know."

She half-shut her eyes. Atwater noticed again that, although her face was much made up, it was well done. He put his arm round her and kissed her. She laughed and lay in his arms and shut her eyes. It was still in the wood, except that now and then they could hear the wash of the sea.

"It's rather nice lying here, isn't it, William?"

"Yes."

"Who are you in love with?"

"No one that you know."

"Don't I?"

"No."

"Do you ever see her?"

"She's gone away."

"Has she?"

"Yes."

She lay in his arms and felt warm and firm as he ran his hand over her body. There was a scent of leaves in the wood and the grass was soft and pleasant to rest on, in spite of all the insects that hummed about over it.

"Who are you in love with?" he said.

"Such a funny man."

"Who?"

"You've never met him. He's a sweet."

"Is he?"

"Yes," she said. "But he lives in Spain."

The air was heavy with the cloying fragrance of the

leaves and there were birds singing near them. The sunlight came through the branches.

"You're a wicked girl, Harriet."

"I know."

He kissed her.

"But what are you doing?" she said.

In the woods things seemed very remote. The insects hummed incessantly round them.

"William."

"Harriet."

"This is silly."

"Not at all."

"Wait a moment."

"That's better."

"Who do these woods belong to?" she said.

He laughed and lay in her arms, kissing her. The universe seemed notably absent.

And then again reality was more contiguous. The birds were still singing a little and they heard the wash of the tide from the direction of the beach. Harriet giggled. She shook her hair.

"Have you a pocket comb?" she said, as she got up.

"Curse you for giggling."

"Have you a comb?"

"No."

I suppose we ought to be getting back."

"Yes."

They made their way out of the wood. It was colder and the noise from the sea was more insistent and there were one or two clouds in the sky. Atwater said:

"We'd better go by the road. It's going to rain."

"Is it?"

"Obviously."

They went through the woods and across a field and out on to the road.

Harriet said: "Don't walk so fast."

"Why not?"

"My shoe hurts."

"Damn your shoe."

She laughed. She said:

"Before you go into the house wipe the lipstick off your face."

As they came near the house large drops of rain began to fall. The sky had become gray. It was going to rain hard.

"We were lucky not to have got caught in that," said Harriet.

Atwater said: "Yes, we were."

## 28

Barlow and Sophy were in the sitting room. They seemed happy and Barlow had done quite a good painting. He showed it to Atwater. Harriet went upstairs to comb her hair. Barlow said:

"You both look very knowing this morning. What have you been doing?"

"We've been on the cliffs watching the sea."

"Was it fun?"

"Not bad."

Atwater sat down on a wooden crate that the claret had arrived in and lit a cigarette. Barlow cleaned some paint off his thumbnail with a rag and turpentine. Harriet came downstairs from combing her hair. She said:

"We saw Raymond bathing. He'd forgotten his towel."

Mrs Race, holding the *Daily Mirror* in her hand, looked through the door.

"Is lunch ready?" she said.

Atwater said: "We're waiting for Raymond. I expect he'll be in soon. We saw him bathing."

Mrs Race sat on the sofa and read the *Daily Mirror.* Sophy darned Barlow's socks and Atwater picked up *Vogue* and opened it, but put it down again and looked out of the window at the rain. Harriet wound up the gramophone. Mrs Race said:

"Poor Raymond is a very bad host, making us wait for him in this way."

She threw the *Daily Mirror* on the ground and sighed. Barlow said:

"I suppose we ought to wait a bit longer."

Mrs Race said: "Have you seen him this morning?"

"Not yet. I went out early to paint. Has anyone spoken to him?"

No one had. Barlow said:

"Do you think it will be awkward?"

He had lost his nerve a little. Mrs Race said:

"It may be very awkward."

"I mean, do you think he will be sticky?"

Mrs Race said: "He always seems to me to be sticky. Sticky and rude."

She had evidently slept badly. She picked up the paper again. They waited, listening to the gramophone. There was no sign of Pringle. Barlow said:

"I think we ought to wait a little longer. In the circumstances."

Harriet said: "Of course he may have got drowned."

"Or had his clothes stolen," said Sophy. "I shouldn't wonder."

"Wouldn't he love it?" said Harriet. She laughed and looked at Atwater, who raised his eyebrows at her.

"He'll have to change all his clothes when he does come in," said Sophy. "He'll be so wet."

They waited. Everyone was hungry. As the clock struck, Mrs Race got up. She said:

"I am now going to lunch. It will be the first meal I

have eaten today, unless you count the aspirin I had at eleven o'clock. The rest of you had better do as you think best."

"Anyway," said Barlow, "we can always sit with him when he does come in. All the food is cold. It's easier to eat lunch late in the afternoon if it's cold lunch."

He was concerned about Pringle. Harriet said:

"Of course it's absurd waiting as late as this for lunch. We'll go in at once."

Atwater followed them into the dining room. The table was laid. The cold beef was at one end of it and there was an envelope on the top of the beef. Harriet said:

"I suppose that's the butcher's bill. Ethel always finds some individual way of drawing our attention to these things."

Barlow reached across the table and took the envelope. He opened it and read the single sheet of paper inside. When he had read it he handed it to Atwater. Atwater read it. Then he read it through again. It was a note from Pringle. It said that he had been depressed for some months. That he felt he had not made a success of his life. And on top of it all was what had happened the night before. He thought, therefore, that he would not come back from bathing in the sea that morning. He asked them to destroy the letter. He added that there were two five-pound notes in the top right-hand drawer of the dressing table beside his bed and would they pay Ethel with one (and give the change to Harriet) and send the other to his sister.

Atwater sat down and read the letter for the third time.

"What do you think?" said Barlow.

Atwater said that he did not know what he thought. He had never seen so clearly as at that moment what a mistake it had been to come and stay in the country with Pringle. He handed the note to Harriet, who was nearest to him. Harriet read it and then read it aloud. Nobody said anything for a short time. There seemed nothing to say that would ease materially the situation. At last Harriet said:

"I don't expect he means it. It's just his inferiority complex coming out, don't you think?"

Sophy was the most surprised. The cinema had accustomed her to violent emotions, but when she realized that Pringle had committed suicide she cried a bit. She knew no details of the night before. Only that Barlow and Pringle had had a row. They often had rows and she and Barlow were going to leave the house on Monday in any case, as she had to be back at work at her shop. But she liked everybody and so she cried a little. Her whole body shook in gentle spasms when she cried.

"I had a premonition that something like this would happen," said Mrs Race. "I knew it all along. I can't imagine why I came."

Barlow said: "I feel entirely to blame."

He looked very, very upset.

Hungry, but thinking it hard to eat while their host's body was driving down the channel, Atwater said:

"What shall we do?"

Mrs Race said: "I refuse to believe that this is not one of his heavy jokes. If we have lunch, I have no doubt he will turn up."

Barlow said: "But, I mean, we can't have lunch."

"Do you propose that we go without food indefinitely?"

Harriet said: "The table is laid. We can eat the food now and call it lunch. Or we can eat it at half-past seven and call it supper."

Mrs Race said: "When we've had some food we shall be more equal to coping with the situation. I feel confident of that."

They sat down and began to eat. There was very little conversation. Atwater was hungry, but by putting the food into his mouth in a disinterested way tried to appear as if he were not eating a lot.

"I think he'll come back," said Harriet; but at the same time she seemed to be rather overawed by circumstances.

Barlow said: "We must get something done about this after lunch."

"May I have the beetroot, Sophy?" said Mrs Race. She looked straight ahead of her. They ate in silence.

Atwater said: "We might go and see if his clothes are there after lunch."

"If he hasn't come back, that is."

Barlow cut them all some bread. Some of Sophy's food went the wrong way and after Harriet had patted her on the back she began to cry again. She borrowed

Barlow's handkerchief as she had forgotten to bring hers down with her and some of the oil paint from it came off on to her face. Barlow said:

"If he doesn't come back I suppose we ought to tell the police."

Atwater peeled the silver paper off his cheese. Mrs Race ate cherries. She was looking incredibly old that day. Barlow said:

"I feel very much to blame."

After lunch they did not make coffee. Pringle's medicine was put by his place at the head of the table and Harriet, when she got up, accidentally upset it and the bottle broke on the floor. They cleared up the bits with the coal-shovel but the medicine stained the rug, which was a special one given to Pringle to work off a bad debt by the man who had designed it.

They waited a little time to digest their food, and then began to walk towards the beach. It was still raining, but not more than a light drizzle and only Mrs Race carried an umbrella. It took longer to reach the place where Pringle had undressed than it had done for Atwater and Harriet to go to the point from where they had seen him, as there was no way down from the cliffs and they had to walk all the way along the shore. The pebbles were slippery from the rain. They went round the small headland that made a sheltered recess of that part of the beach. The clothes were still there and very wet from the rain. They walked up to them and looked at them. Sophy held a handkerchief that she had taken the precaution of bringing with her. Atwater said:

"Are we going to take them back?"

"What do you think?"

Mrs Race said: "We'd better take them back."

Everybody took a garment. Harriet took the trousers, which she carried slung over her shoulder by the braces attached to them and Sophy held all the odds and ends that were tiresome to carry. They went back over the slippery stones along the shore to the house. Barlow was upset. He kept on saying:

"You know, this is all my fault."

Mrs Race said: "If you say that again I shall strike you."

"I suppose we ought to tell someone about this."

Atwater said: "Who? And what are we to tell them?"

"The police or something."

Mrs Race said: "Who ever heard of anyone going to the police outside a detective story? What could they do, anyway?"

"Especially as he wants it to appear an accident," said Atwater.

Harriet said: "He probably swam round the corner of the cliff and walked all the way to the Bungalow Hotel and stayed there just to give us a fright."

But she did not seem to think that this was what Pringle had done, although she said so. Atwater said:

"Anyway, the car is still out of order. We'll tell someone about it when we go into the town tomorrow on our way back."

After that no one talked.

When they arrived at the house they put Pringle's

soggy clothes in his room. Atwater wondered why Pringle had put on a suit if he were going to drown himself. He often wore only shorts and a shirt, but for some reason today he had put a lot of clothes on, as Atwater supposed, to give more trouble. In any case, he might just as well have gone in wearing his clothes, whatever they were. The damp clothes smelt disagreeable and Atwater shut the door of the bedroom after him. Mrs Race said she was going to lie down. Atwater went downstairs, where he found Ethel clearing away the remains of lunch. When Atwater paid her she seemed sorry to hear that her job was coming to an end. Harriet took the change and went up to her room to write a letter to some Jews she knew in Leicestershire who would probably put her up for a week or two. Atwater sat down and began to draft a letter to Pringle's sister, who was married to one of the directors of an oil company. Atwater remembered that Pringle had always said how odd she considered him, so he thought she would probably be not too surprised to get the letter. He hoped, anyway, that it would not come as a shock. He read the letter he wrote to Barlow before he sealed it up with the second five-pound note inside. He supposed that however rich people were they were glad to receive an unexpected five pounds.

## 29

The Sunday afternoon passed slowly and with the hours
it was easier to become accustomed to the idea of
Pringle's suicide. After another heavy downpour the
rain had stopped. It was warm, so that steam came up
from the soaked lawn and water dripped off laurel
bushes. The tennis net, which no one had taken the
trouble to lift off the ground nor even to slacken, had
begun to sag on the grass. Barlow and Sophy were in
the garden talking about plans for getting home. It was
a Sunday afternoon of traditional usage, with church
bells sounding a long way off, melancholy, across the
fields. Atwater sat in the house and read *Trilby,* which
Barlow had recently given Sophy as a birthday present.
He had read it before, but now it seemed to be the book
for the circumstances, and, although the conduct of its
characters struck a familiar note, it was one that was
not too painful to bear. As he was reading, Mrs Race
came in. She still looked her full age, but although she
had been lying down she had tidied her hair and was
on the whole less disheveled than she had been earlier
in the afternoon. She said:

"Did you know our late host at all well?"

"I've known him for about three years."

"Are you surprised at this?"

"Not particularly."

"I am very, very angry," said Mrs Race. "Very angry. I could smack Harriet. But if it had not been her it would have been someone else. One must face that."

"I'm very sorry it's happened," Atwater said, not seeing why he should enlarge on his feelings for Naomi Race.

"Of course, *anyone* might get drowned," said Mrs Race.

"Anyone."

"Did you say that to his sister?"

"More or less."

"You destroyed his note?"

"Yes."

"I suppose we ought to report this some time."

"We can do that when we go into the town tomorrow. We can't go tonight. The car isn't working."

"Anyway, there's nothing to be done when we do tell them."

"Who do we tell?" said Atwater. "The policeman on point duty?"

"What are you doing for the rest of your holiday?"

"I was going back to work tomorrow, in any case."

"You might have missed this altogether."

Mrs Race sighed.

"No one has been very considerate," she said.

"No."

"Where are the others?"

"Sophy and Barlow are in the garden. Harriet is writing letters upstairs."

"I shall go for a short walk and try and clear my brain."

Atwater continued to read *Trilby* and Mrs Race went away on her walk. He read for some time. Then he put the book down. Psychologically it was interesting, he thought, that Little Billee should have derived so much pleasure from working men's clubs and a great pity that Pringle had not been able to find an unobjectionable relaxation of a similar sort. Poor old Pringle. He had all the worst points of Little Billee and Svengali combined, without any of the former's worldly success or the latter's hypnotic powers. On the other hand, he had a more amusing circle of friends than they had had. It was a pity in a way that he was gone. He was still thinking about them all, and how Pringle would have importuned Trilby herself if he had known her, when Barlow came in from the garden. Sophy was not with him. He said:

"What are your feelings about this?"

"I think it was a very silly thing to do."

"Do you think it was my fault?"

Atwater stood up. He felt suddenly as if he were going to be sick. All he wanted was to leave at once before he followed Pringle into the sea. But he said:

"Has the man come to mend the car?"

"No. He said he might be late."

"Will he come?"

"He's what's known as a reliable man."

"Then we shall be able to get away tomorrow?"

"Ought we to take the car in this evening and tell someone he hasn't come back and that we've found his clothes?"

"Take the car in if you like when it's mended."

"I can't drive."

"Neither can I."

"How are we going to get away tomorrow then?"

"Harriet has got to take us. Or be strangled."

"Oughtn't she to go in tonight?"

"I should suggest it to her if I were you."

"Shall I?"

"If it would make you happier."

"Would she go?"

"Is it likely?"

"The Chalks will look after the house until his sister turns up."

"Yes."

Barlow said: "I'm not really surprised that he did it."

"We shall have to garage the car somewhere near the station and leave it there," said Atwater.

"That was a very good letter you wrote his sister."

"She always expected that something of the sort would happen."

"So have I," said Barlow. "But it's absurd that I should have been the cause of it. I mean he always seemed to like me."

"I almost agree with Naomi Race. She says he's let us all down."

"Does she say that?"

"More or less."

"Of course, that's what he has done in a way."

"You agree?"

"But then I feel I've behaved badly to Sophy again.

Of course I suppose I ought to marry her really. But what would you have done if you'd found yourself similarly placed with Harriet?"

"It seems unprofitable to discuss hypothetical situations of that kind. I think you behaved unwisely."

"But what would you have done?"

"I really have no idea."

"I expect you'd have been just as unwise."

"That must remain a matter of opinion."

"Do you think it would be a good thing if I settled down and married Miriam?"

"It might have saved a lot of trouble once. Now it's too late."

Barlow said: "Oh, you never know. It's just the sort of thing that might happen again."

"Do you think so?"

"After all, one must face facts."

"I'm very sorry it has happened."

"Sophy is very upset."

"I'm not surprised."

"What an ass I was," said Barlow. "I wish it had never happened. Anyway, I don't expect Miriam would have me."

Atwater sat down again. He still felt far from well, but the sudden nausea had passed. Barlow said:

"I shall go out in the garden again until supper. Are you coming?"

"No."

"And we will tell them about it in the town tomorrow morning?"

"All right."

"What are you doing?"

"I'm reading a book."

Barlow went away. Atwater poured out a lot of soda water and drank it. Then he poured out some more and drank that. He hated them all and only wanted to see Susan again. Where the devil had she gone? As for Harriet...He took out his cigarette case but it was empty. The room was still untidy and he searched for the cigarette box that was usually there. Unable to find it, he gave up the search and sat down again and thought. After concentration on the problem it became evident that the cigarette box was in the dining room and he went across the passage. The dining room door was shut and someone was moving about inside the room. Atwater listened. Then he went in. He was not wholly surprised to see Pringle standing by the table; but he wondered why Pringle was wearing a fisherman's jumper, corduroy trousers, and wading boots. Atwater closed the door behind him. Pringle had one hand on the table and was looking round the room. Atwater said:

"Hullo."

"Hullo," said Pringle. He did not look up.

"Are you looking for anything?"

Pringle turned round. He seemed tired. He said:

"I wrote a letter and left it on the table before I went out this morning."

"Did you leave it on the beef?"

"Yes."

238

"I'm afraid we destroyed it."

"You read it?"

"Yes."

"Everyone?"

"Yes."

"I decided not to," said Pringle. "I was picked up by some men in a boat. That's why I'm dressed like this."

"We brought back your clothes," said Atwater. He felt embarrassed. Pringle looked so tired. Pringle said:

"I hope you were careful of my wristwatch. It was in one of the pockets of the coat."

"Sophy put some salad oil in the works. It was rather wet."

"Who broke my medicine?"

"Harriet."

"On purpose?"

"No. By accident. I'm afraid it's made rather a mess of the rug."

"It's ruined it."

"Yes, it has."

"I decided against suicide on the whole," said Pringle.

"We were all very worried."

"As it happened, there were a lot of boats about. But some of them would take no notice of me."

"I wrote to your sister. But I have not posted it. I paid Ethel. Harriet has got the change."

"One of the men in another boat said that he was going to report me to the police for bathing without a bathing dress."

Pringle looked on his last legs. All the clothes he was

wearing were too big for him. His red hair was horrible. Atwater said:

"I expect you'd like something to eat. Shall I get Sophy to make you some Bovril?"

Before Pringle could answer there was a sound of humming outside. Atwater stepped away from the door as it opened and Harriet came in. She stopped in the doorway.

"Hullo, Raymond," she said. "Why are you dressed like that? Are you going to a party? Can we come too?"

She went across the room and put both her hands on Pringle's shoulders and then put her head down on his chest. She remained like that for a few seconds.

"How funny you smell," she said.

Pringle put both his arms round her and lowered his head on to hers.

"You are an old silly," she said.

He went out of the room and left Pringle and Harriet together. He went into the garden. Barlow and Sophy were sitting in deck chairs in the far corner of the lawn. Sophy was mending underclothes and Barlow had his copy of *Thus Spake Zarathustra* with him, but he was not reading it. Atwater said:

"Raymond is back. He's dressed like a fisherman."

Barlow got up quickly from his chair.

"Is he?"

"Yes, he is."

"Thank goodness. You know, I felt much to blame about all that."

Barlow sighed and began to relight his pipe.

"Very much to blame," he said.

"I thought he'd come back," said Sophy. She smiled. "Didn't you, William?" she said.

"Yes," said Atwater, "I did."

"Thank goodness he's back," said Barlow. He sat down again.

Sophy said: "But why is he dressed like a fisherman?"

Mrs Race, returning from her walk, came towards them across the lawn. She was carrying a Y-shaped stick and looked like one of the witches out of a performance of *Macbeth* in modern dress. When she was close to them Atwater said:

"He's back."

"Who is?"

"Raymond."

"Do you mean he's still alive?"

"He's in the dining room talking to Harriet."

Mrs Race said: "Give me a cigarette. And get up, Hector. I want to sit in that chair."

"But why is he dressed like a fisherman?" said Sophy.

## 30

"Has he gone to bed?" said Atwater.

Harriet said: "He's finished the Bovril. He'll be asleep soon. He's tired."

"I shall go to bed soon myself," said Atwater. "I shall let my supper settle first."

"It's been a tiring day," said Mrs Race. "I must say I was surprised when you told me he'd come back."

Harriet said: "We're going up to London with you all tomorrow. We both think some London life would do us good for a short time."

"How long did he take this place for?" said Barlow.

"All the summer. We may come back again later on."

Mrs Race said: "I expect London will still be very empty. But I think you're wise to leave here for a bit."

They were in the sitting room, smoking. The wind had risen a little from the sea and made a draught along one side of the loom. There was knocking on the outside door. Sophy put down her work, a pair of Barlow's pants, and went to see who it was. Barlow said:

"The weather seems to have broken at the moment. But it may clear up later."

Sophy came back to the sitting room. She said:

"The man has come to take the clothes back."

"What clothes?"

"The clothes they lent Raymond."

Harriet said: "They're in the bathroom."

Sophy said: "Oh, I'll get them," and went toward the door.

Barlow said:

"Is he waiting outside?"

"Yes."

"I suppose we ought to give him something."

Yes," said Atwater, "we ought."

"How much do you think we ought to give him, Naomi?"

Mrs Race said: "Well, what exactly did he do?"

Harriet said: "One of them lifted Raymond out of the water. But we don't know whether it was this man or not."

"What else?"

"They lent him the clothes he came back in."

"Was that all?"

"More or less."

Mrs Race said: "As regards the loan of the clothes, I should say half-a-crown was ample."

"The point is," said Barlow, "that they lifted him out of the water too."

Mrs Race said: "Why not make it up to ten shillings."

Barlow said: "I'm not sure that seven and six is really enough for that." He said to Atwater: "How much do you think?"

"We ought really to ask Raymond himself, I suppose."

Sophy came in with the clothes. She said:

"Here they are. Big boots and a jumper and these trousers."

She stood holding them, dragged over to one side by the weight of the seaboots she was carrying. Harriet said:

"Could you hear if Raymond was asleep when you were upstairs?"

"I didn't hear anything."

Sophy put the boots on the floor.

"Shall I give them to the man?" she said.

Mrs Race said: "Did Raymond tell you anything about what they did for him when they took him out of the sea, Sophy?"

"They just lifted him out," said Sophy. "He said they hurt him getting him over the side of the boat."

"The man outside," said Barlow, "what sort of a man is he?"

"He's a tall man."

Barlow stood up.

"What do you think?" he said.

Harriet said: "Why not go and ask Raymond. I don't expect he's asleep yet."

"You go, then."

Mrs Race said: "I think ten shillings would be quite enough."

Harriet said: "Even if it is only ten shillings, we must get it from Raymond."

"I've got two pounds," Barlow said, "but it has to last me till Friday. Besides, I haven't any ten-shilling notes."

Atwater said: "But do you think that ten shillings is enough? I doubt it."

"I don't think it is," said Harriet. "After all, Raymond put them all to a lot of trouble. I expect this man has walked over a long way too."

"I think about a pound."

Harriet said: "Let's give him a drink while we're discussing it. Go and ask him what he'd like, Sophy."

Sophy went out to ask the man what he'd like. Barlow said:

"I think you'd better ask Raymond, Harriet."

Atwater said: "I've got a pound, if you think that would be the right sum. I could get it back from Raymond later."

"Personally," said Mrs Race, "it seems to me too much. Especially as Raymond is returning here later on. It may happen again."

Sophy came back. She said:

"He's a teetotaler. But he says he'd like a cup of cocoa."

"Have we got any cocoa?"

"No," said Sophy. "Shall I make him some coffee?"

Barlow said: "Yes, make him some coffee. But don't make it in the machine. It takes too long."

Sophy left the room again and they heard her put the kettle on. Mrs Race said:

"It would really be better to ask Raymond himself."

Harriet said: "Why don't you go and ask him, William?"

"If someone has got to wake him up it would probably come better from you."

"All right," said Harriet, "I'll go and ask him. But

he's annoyed about my having broken that medicine bottle. He seems to think I did it on purpose."

She went upstairs. Mrs Race said:

"This sort of question is always so difficult to settle. Afterwards one always feels one has given either too much or too little."

Barlow said: "I think ten shillings is really too little. On the other hand, a pound seems a lot. You see, they only picked him out of the water."

Atwater said: "They have probably got the whole incident out of all proportion to its importance, in their minds, by this time. You must remember that."

Sophy looked through the door.

"Shall I ask the man how many lumps of sugar he likes?" she said. Barlow said:

"Yes, ask him that."

They heard Harriet's voice on the stairs. She came in. Pringle, wearing black pajamas and a very old Jaeger dressing gown, was with her. His eyes were almost shut and strands of red hair protruded unevenly from his head. He was carrying a notecase in one hand. Harriet said:

"He couldn't understand what it was all about, so I thought he'd better come down and see the man himself."

"Who is this man?" said Pringle. He rubbed his eyes.

Mrs Race said: "He's the man who lent you the clothes. We thought you'd like to give him some money."

"What clothes?"

"The clothes you came back from the sea in. Don't you want to give him some money?"

"Why?"

"I don't know."

Pringle said: "Well, if you all think so, I suppose I ought. How much shall I give him?"

Mrs Race said: "I think ten shillings would be enough. The others think a pound."

"Ten shillings?" said Pringle. "A pound?"

Atwater said: "You see, they've probably got the whole thing out of proportion in their minds."

"But, I mean, a pound is enormous."

"Give him ten shillings, then."

"Ten shillings isn't enough," said Harriet. "You must see that."

Atwater said: "How many men were there?"

"Two," said Pringle. "But only one of them helped me into the boat."

Mrs Race said: "Why not compromise and give the man fifteen shillings?"

Pringle said: "I might do that." He looked as if he had woken up now. He fumbled about in his notecase.

"Has anyone got any change?" he said.

Barlow said: "I can give you half-a-crown, but it's the only loose change I've got. The two pounds has got to last me till Friday."

"Here's another half-crown," said Atwater. "So, if you've got ten shillings?"

Sophy came in again.

"He's drinking the coffee," she said.

She sat down and went on with her work. Pringle said:

"Will you give him this, Sophy?"

He gave her a ten-shilling note and the two half-crowns. Sophy took the money and went out again. When she came back, carrying the coffee cup, Mrs Race said:

"What did he say?"

Sophy said: "He just said, 'Tar'."

"Nothing more?"

"No."

"That was obviously the right sum," said Pringle and, retying his dressing gown cord, he went upstairs. He said:

"And don't disturb me again. I don't care who it is. I won't see them."

"He's getting back to his old form," said Barlow.

Mrs Race said: "A few days in London will soon put him right."

## 31

"What was the country like?" said Nosworth. He looked more yellow than he had done when Atwater had gone away. Atwater said:

"Much the same as usual. We had some nice weather."

"I've mentioned that question of the revolving chair to Spurgeon and he's going to put it before the standing committee."

"Thanks."

"Don't thank me. It was my duty."

"Has anything happened in London?"

Nosworth shook his head. There were a few letters on Atwater's desk. The first three were bills for books and the next a note from Verelst, saying that he was going abroad and giving the name of a hotel in France that he said he had forgotten to let Atwater have before. The next one was a bright blue envelope, fussily addressed in Lola's handwriting. He opened it. Nosworth said:

"Dr Crutch has been here several times since you've been away."

Atwater read Lola's letter through again. So that was all over. He was sorry in a way. He made a note on his pad to answer it and thought how she must have enjoyed composing a letter of that kind.

"How has he been keeping?" he said.

"There was a noticeable change for the worse the last time he came."

"Was there?" said Atwater. He put Lola's letter in his pocket. Nosworth said:

"It was a pity you forgot to give him back that brochure. However, I told him that you were returning today and he said he'd look in."

"Really."

"Yes. I expect he'll be in some time this afternoon."

"How are Miller's varicose veins?"

"He's still away on and off. And there's a new rule that exhibits are to be dusted on every alternate Monday. Could you supervise that?"

"Including the Mark III cases?"

"Yes," said Nosworth, "including the Mark III cases."

"What does Spurgeon think about that?"

"Naturally he's very put out. However, he's compromised by refusing to do his share of correcting the proofs of the septennial catalogue."

"I admire him for that."

"After all, a time does come when a protest must be lodged."

"We're not the standing committee's coolies."

"Just at this time when one is so busy."

"It's very unreasonable."

Nosworth said: "I have all those Danish poems to translate and then I'm doing an introduction to a *catalogue raisonné* of the Palmanini Collection."

"When is that appearing?"

"In the autumn," said Nosworth. "And by the way, one two people have rung you up recently. Female voices."

"How many?"

"Oh, quite a few. But I refused to give them your address."

"Did they leave any message?"

"One of them said something about saying good-bye."

"Do you know what her name was?"

"I don't at all."

"Anything else?"

"That Czech has made a lot of trouble."

"Trouble?"

"Extra work," said Nosworth. "Extra work."

He went into his own room. The boy with the cauliflower ear came in.

"Dr Crutch to see you," he said, and moved what he was eating from one side of his mouth to the other.

"Show him into the waiting room."

Atwater turned toward the waiting room and Dr Crutch. It was quite a long interview. Later in the morning he wrote to Lola, his bank manager, and several letters about ethnography. Then he rang up Susan. Old Nunnery answered the telephone in a thick undertone and said Susan was away.

"Come in and see me, anyway," he said, and coughed horribly down the line.

"When?"

"About nine or ten tonight."

"I will."

"Do," said old Nunnery. "There may be something to drink."

## 32

The outside door was shut. Atwater rang the bell several times, but nothing happened. Then he went out into the road and looked up towards the Nunnerys' flat. There was a moon, so that it was fairly light and as he was looking he saw Mr Nunnery's head appear.

"Sorry," shouted Mr Nunnery. "The catch must have slipped. I'll throw the key down."

He disappeared. Atwater waited. Mr Nunnery came back after a few minutes and leant far out so that he could see over the coping running along the upper part of the house. From below it seemed that he would certainly lose his balance.

"Coming down," he shouted. His voice sounded far away, unexpected, like a message from the firmament. He shouted "Coming down" again and Atwater thought that nothing was more likely. The key, wrapped in a page of the *Morning Post,* sailed slowly down from the vault of stars and landed on the head of a blind man, tapping his way along the railings of the area. Atwater tried to explain, but it took too long, so he gave the blind man a shilling and went up the stairs. Mephitic vapors hung like a mist over the lower flights, lessening in intensity as he reached the upper landing. The flat door was open. He walked in and put his hat in the hall and knocked on the sitting room door.

"Come in," shouted Mr Nunnery. He was sitting alone and drinking a glass of port while he did a crossword puzzle. He had the look of being rather ashamed of himself.

"Hullo, Atwater," he said. "Have a drink."

He fetched another glass from the cupboard and poured out some port into it.

"Have you been away?" he said.

"I've been in the country. It was rather nice."

"I don't care for the country," said Mr Nunnery. "Were you staying with people?"

"With Raymond Pringle."

"The man with red hair who always used to be ringing Susan up?"

"Yes. The man with red hair."

"Has he a nice place?"

"No."

"How was he?"

"He seemed fairly well when I left."

"I expect he'll kill himself one of these days," said Mr Nunnery. He looks as if he would."

"Yes, I expect he will."

"Have some more of this," said Mr Nunnery and added: "Of whimsical design? Seven letters?"

"Baroque?"

"That's it."

"Is it?"

"Certainly."

Atwater said: "How is Susan?"

"As far as I know she's all right."

Mr Nunnery did not seem altogether at his best that evening. Atwater thought it possible that he was in a state of well-controlled drunkenness, which made him rather ponderous. Atwater said:

"I haven't seen her for some time."

"She's been away. She still is."

"Really."

"She's gone to America."

"America?"

"America," said Mr Nunnery. "With that fellow Verelst."

"Oh, yes?"

"Yes," said Mr Nunnery. "Not a companion I should have chosen myself. But there it is."

"I haven't seen her for some time."

"Of course, she's always wanted to go to America."

"I remember her saying so."

Mr Nunnery said: "He's all right, Verelst, really."

"Oh, yes."

"I don't dislike him because he's a Jew," said Mr Nunnery. "One can't dismiss whole races at a time."

"He's all right."

"You'd hardly know he was a Jew."

"Oh no. Hardly at all."

"Still, there are people I should have preferred her to go to America with."

"I see what you mean."

Atwater felt a little as if the pit of his stomach were going to drop out. He still did not believe. It was obviously nonsense. The old fool was drunk.

"Have some port," said Mr Nunnery, who seemed relieved to have got the information about Susan off his chest. He said:

"You look depressed. You're probably like me. The country doesn't suit you."

"I'm all right."

"It's not what you'd call very good port," said Mr Nunnery. "It came out of a bottle that Fotheringham left when he came here the other night."

"How is he?"

"Remarkably well. But he may be losing his job."

"The usual job?"

"I suppose you'd call it the usual job."

Atwater said: "I'm sorry I didn't see Susan again before she went."

Mr Nunnery said: "It was all rather sudden, you know. She likes doing things on the spur of the moment."

"Do you think Fotheringham will lose his job?"

"If they've stood him for five years, I for one see no reason why they should not stand him for fifty."

"Has he anything in mind?"

"An American called Scheigan held out some hope of employment."

"I know Scheigan. He's a publisher."

"Unfortunately, nothing is ever decided when they go out together."

"Fotheringham wants something intellectual."

"Nothing ever gets decided, as I say."

"Scheigan has no decision."

Mr Nunnery emptied the dregs of the decanter into Atwater's glass. He said:

"In my opinion Scheigan drinks too much."

Atwater said: "Has Susan gone to live over there permanently?"

"Oh no. I think she'll be back soon. I hope so at least."

There was a pause. Atwater did not even try to think of something to say. Mr Nunnery said:

"Who else was staying at Pringle's that I know?"

"Do you know Naomi Race?"

"Of course, I used to in the old days."

"Barlow?"

"Oh, yes, he paints."

"Harriet Twining?"

"There's a girl I like," said Mr Nunnery. "How was she?"

"Very well."

"It sounds a very gay party."

"It was."

There was another pause. Atwater wondered whether it was the port that made him feel like that. Mr Nunnery blinked. He said:

"What do you think the winter is going to be like?"

"Bad."

"Yes. So do I. Bad."

Atwater said: "Verelst knows America well, doesn't he?"

"I believe he made some of his money there."

"I should like to go there myself."

"So should I," said Mr Nunnery. "On Wall Street

something might be done. There are some thrusters there, not the wretched pack of old women on the Stock Market over here."

Atwater said: "I shall have to be leaving now."

He felt suddenly that he couldn't stay a moment longer.

"For goodness' sake don't go."

"Yes, I must go."

"Well, if you must," said Mr Nunnery, "you must. I'm sorry there's no more port."

"Good-bye."

"Good-bye," said Mr Nunnery. "Come in again soon. I'm afraid they may cut the telephone off tomorrow or the next day, as I haven't paid the account. But I'm usually in about this time."

"Good-bye again."

"Wait a moment. What was the word you said?"

"Baroque."

"Was it?"

"You said so."

"That was it," said Mr Nunnery. "I'll write it down at once in case I forget it again."

## 33

Atwater went down the evil-smelling stairs. He went into the street and walked for a long way, thinking what a pity it was that he could not remember what Susan looked like. Now she was gone and he could not see her he wanted to imagine that he was going to meet her soon again, but all he could remember was the color of her dress when he had seen her first, and when he tried to imagine her the dress itself faded into a blur and he was left without anything of her at all. They had written each other no letters, but he thought of the inflections of her voice on the telephone, so that all the things she had said lost with the different tones he gave them any meaning that they once had had. And so she was gone, ridiculous, lovely creature, absurdly hopeless and impossible love who was and had always been so far away. Absurdly lovely, hopeless creature who was gone away so that he would never see her again and would only remember her as an absurdly hopeless love. He walked twice round the same square. He became tired of walking and took a bus that had slowed down near him. He went on top and sat on one of the front seats She had gone to America with Verelst. He watched the trees of the park through the open window on his left. Or had that drunken old fool of a father got muddled? Perhaps she had not gone away at all. He became tired of the bus and got off it and began to walk again. He thought of all the times that he might have been with her or near her when he had chosen to do something different. Or when he had just done nothing. When he had just sat in his room and read a book when he might have been talking to her on the telephone. But then there were also all the times when he had tried to be with her and she had wanted to be with someone else. The times when she had been out or bored or not kept the appointment or even had not been looking her best. She was right, he supposed, to leave him and to go away. And that bastard Verelst, who really wasn't so bad. And yet how ridiculous and impossible it was to think that she had gone away. While he had sat yawning in the museum or bickering with Pringle or making love to Lola or Harriet or some other dismal woman at some dismal party she had been with Verelst and now she had gone with him to America. What a fool he'd been. What a fool. And yet, as she had said, what would the good have been? But in spite of it all he could only think of the time he had wasted when she had not been with him and the other time, that now seemed the only time when he had been alive at all, and the time before him now when she would not be with him and he could not even see her or be near her or talk to her or look at her and when all he would hear of her would be what the wretched people one knew said as they gossiped and chattered and speculated about the other wretched people's love affairs. For now she had gone away. There had been meetings when he had felt that the whole thing had been a silly mistake and that she was not like what he thought she was like and he had not enjoyed being with her. But always when she had gone he had known that he was wrong and it was his imaginary picture of her that was real and her own reality the illusion. He came to Hyde Park Corner and thought that the thing simply couldn't be true. And yet why shouldn't it be true? If she hadn't actually told him in so many words that something like it was going to happen she had given him a very fair indication. What an ass he'd been. As for Verelst and his damned letter about some damned hotel. Anyway she was gone now. He began to walk up Piccadilly. How impossible it was to think of London without her. And yet he'd only known her about five minutes. What had he done in the days before they had met? Or was it that filthy port that made him feel so ill?

It was a clear night and heavy men in dinner jackets were strolling back from dinner at their clubs. Atwater went up Piccadilly. At one of the street corners a young man in a bowler hat, carrying an unrolled umbrella, was standing in consultation with several women. As Atwater passed, the young man put out the crook of his umbrella and with it caught him by the arm. Atwater glanced at him and saw that it was Fotheringham. Fotheringham said:

"Hullo, William. I'm going to be an awful bore. I'm going to ask you to lend me ten bob."

"Are you?"

"Can you be an absolute good Samaritan?"

"I think so."

Fotheringham put the note in his trouser pocket. He took out a cigarette case and offered it to Atwater. He said:

"I've just been having dinner with one of the directors of a small shipping firm. He may be going to give me a job."

"May he?"

"Awful, it was."

"Where did you dine?"

"At his club. It was terrible. A very bad club. No traditions. I can't tell you what the food was like. However, it may mean a job."

"Yes?"

"Yes. And where have you been at this time of night, may I ask? Or would it be indiscreet?"

"I've just been seeing old Nunnery."

"I was in there the other night," said Fotheringham. "I was looking at some photographs of Susan he had there. You know, she's a very attractive girl."

"Yes, she is."

"I never know whether she or Harriet Twining is the more attractive."

"You said so once before."

"In a subtle sort of way, I think Harriet."

Atwater said: "Oh, do you? I think I prefer Susan."

Fotheringham said: "Well, it's a matter one can't decide by arguing." He said: "The last few hours have been pretty heavy going for me."

"I expect so."

"I feel as if I'd just come out of my housemaster's

room after a talk on *esprit-de-corps*. In short, I need cheering up."

"Now dear," said one of the women, "don't go on chin wagging all night." She was wearing a heavy fur coat, as the night was fresh, although not really cold.

"I'm sorry, I'm sorry," said Fotheringham. "I'll be with you in two seconds, Ivy."

He said to Atwater:

"It looks as if I shall have to go."

"Don't let me keep you."

"Well, ten thousand thanks again, William. And I'll let you have that ten bob back some time. We might have a drink together on Friday."

"I can't on Friday. Monday?"

"No. Monday is never a good day for me. But I'll post it to you tomorrow."

"Do."

"I will," said Fotheringham. "I will." He disappeared up White Horse Street.

"Won't you come for a little walk with me, dear?" said an elderly woman in a very tight small hat. She had been one of the group round Fotheringham.

"No, thanks," said Atwater, "I have troubles of my own."

"In business yourself, I shouldn't wonder," she said.

Atwater said: "It will come to that soon, I expect," and went on up Piccadilly, stopping at Heppell's to buy some toothpaste. The night was certainly colder than it had been for some months and it occurred to him that it would soon be autumn. He turned into Soho and went through several side streets.

"Haven't seen you for some time, sir," said the porter as Atwater came through the door.

"No," said Atwater, "you haven't."

The porter belched quietly to himself behind his hand and said: "Manners." Atwater took the check for his hat and went into the bar. It was almost empty, but Pringle was sitting at the far end round the corner. He was looking annoyed. He said:

"Fancy coming here your first night in London."

"What about you?"

"You don't suppose it was my choice."

"Where is Harriet?"

"She's found some young man and has been dancing with him the whole evening."

"Has she?"

"He seems to expect me to buy all his drinks."

Atwater said he was sorry to hear it. He sat down at one of the tables at the side of the room.

"I want a kipper," he said to the waiter. "And if it's too late for a drink bring me a large black coffee." He was not specially hungry, but he had forgotten to have any dinner and eating a kipper would be something to do. Pringle brought his drink over from the bar and sat at the table. He said:

"Undershaft is back. He was here tonight."

"How was he?"

"Palsied."

"Celebrating his return?"

"That must have been it."

Atwater ate his kipper. Walter Brisket came in with a very German fair young man wearing a tartan bowtie.

"Hullo, William," he said.

"Hullo."

Brisket said: "Do you know the Freiherr von Waldesch?"

Atwater shook hands. Von Waldesch put his head a little to one side and stroked the hair at the back of his head, which he wore short. Evidently the victim of central heating, he looked unhealthy to a degree, but he was a heavily-built young man and had one good dueling scar. Brisket said:

"I'm afraid he doesn't talk much English, poor dear, but he's all right really."

Pringle said: "Have you both been upstairs?"

"It was so dull, we came down here."

"Is Harriet still up there?" said Pringle.

"Yes. Dancing with something very special."

Pringle said: "Undershaft says America is an astonishing country. They call bowler hats 'derbies.' There isn't such a thing as a public lavatory, as such, in the whole of New York."

Atwater finished his kipper and pushed the plate away.

"You have to drink whisky all the time, don't you?"

"He says there's plenty of gin if you don't like whisky."

"How long has Undershaft been back?"

"About a week or ten days."

Pringle said: "He hasn't taken long to get a new girl."

"Hasn't he?"

"She's called Lola."

Atwater said: "What happened to the Annamite?"

"This new girl," said Pringle, "says she knows you. She told Undershaft she thought it so funny the way you mended your braces with wire."

"Did she?"

"Yes. Undershaft says she's nice."

"She is."

"He says she's tiresome in a way, but attractive."

"Does he?"

Brisket said: "For heaven's sake, leave off talking about women and tell us something amusing."

"Undershaft met Scheigan when he was in New York. He fell over him when he was coming back from a party in Greenwich Village."

"And then?"

"Later Scheigan said he knew all of us."

"Did he send any messages?"

"He specially asked Undershaft to tell Harriet that he wanted his gold cigarette case back."

Von Waldesch, getting rather bored, took out a toothpick, but did not venture on more than a cursory excavation. Brisket ordered him some coffee to keep him quiet. Von Waldesch sat there smiling to himself with a sort of self-possessed shyness rather like Sophy's. Brisket said:

"Undershaft saw Susan Nunnery in America."

"How was she?" said Atwater. He wondered if he

was talking about a real person or someone he had once read about or seen a picture of. It was a million years since he had been with her.

"She was with a man called Verelst."

"I know him."

"You know her, of course?"

"She's very attractive in her way," said Brisket. "But too individual to be *chic* really."

Atwater said: "How was she getting on with Verelst?"

Harriet came down the stairs. She was holding the arm of a tall young man whom Atwater had not seen before.

"That is a very nice young man," she said. "I don't know what his name is, but he says a friend of his is giving a party and we can all come."

"Yes," said the young man, rather frightened by his own sudden importance, "do come, all of you. I don't expect it will be very exciting or anything like that, but all the same we might look in and see what it's like."

Atwater said: "How was Susan Nunnery getting on with Verlest?"

Brisket said: "This is the Freiherr von Waldesch, Harriet. Have you met him?"

Harriet said: "You'll come to the party, won't you?"

Von Waldesch bowed from the waist.

"Very well," he said. He looked immensely pleased by the invitation and a little alarmed by Harriet. By way of additional emphasis to his acceptance he said: "That's right."

"And you, William?"

"Yes," said Atwater, "I'd like to."

# ANTHONY POWELL

Born in London in 1905, Anthony Powell is one of the great figures of Twentieth Century British fiction. After graduating from Balliol College, Oxford, he began publishing fiction. His early books include *Afternoon Men* (1931), *Venusberg* (1932), *From a View to a Death* (1933), *Agents and Patients* (1936), and *What's Become of Waring* (1939).

In the 1940s Powell worked primarily on an anthology on John Aubrey and his friends, and wrote a biography of that author. In the early 1950s Powell began his great twelve volume series, *A Dance to the Music of Time,* which was completed in 1982.

*O, How the Wheel Becomes It!* was published in 1983. He is also the author of two plays and a four volume memoir, *To Keep the Ball Rolling.*

Powell has been awarded numerous literary prizes, including the James Tait Black Prize, the W.H. Smith Award, The Hudson Review Bennett Award, the T.S. Eliot Prize for Creative Writing, and an Ingersoll Foundation award. He lives in Somerset, England.

THOMAS MANN [Germany]
  *Six Early Stories* 109  (1-55713-298-4, $22.95)

F. T. MARINETTI [Italy]
  *Let's Murder the Moonshine: Selected Writings* 12
    (1-55713-101-5, $13.95)
  *The Untameables* 28  (1-55713-044-7, $10.95)

HARRY MATHEWS [USA]
  *Selected Declarations of Dependence* (1-55713-234-8, $10.95)

DOUGLAS MESSERLI [USA]
  Ed. *50: A Celebration of Sun & Moon Classics* 50
    (1-55713-132-5, $13.95)
  Ed. *From the Other Side of the Century: A New American
    Poetry 1960–1990* 47  (1-55713-131-7, $29.95)

CHRISTOPHER MORLEY [USA]
  *Thunder on the Left* 68  (1-55713-190-2, $12.95)

CEES NOOTEBOOM [The Netherlands]
  *The Captain of the Butterflies* 97  (1-55713-315-8, $11.95)

VALÈRE NOVARINA [France]
  *The Theater of the Ears* 85  (1-55713-251-8, $13.95)

MICHAEL PALMER, RÉGIS BONVICINO, and
  NELSON ASCHER, EDS. [USA and Brazil]
  *Nothing the Sun Could Not Explain: 20 Contemporary Brazilian Poets*
    82  (1-55713-366-2, $15.95)

ANTHONY POWELL [England]
  *O, How the Wheel Becomes It!* 76  (1-55713-221-6, $10.95)
  *Afternoon Men* 108  (1-55713-284-4, $10.95)

SEXTUS PROPERTIUS [Ancient Rome]
  *Charm* 89  (1-55713-224-0, $11.95)

CARL RAKOSI [USA]
  *Poems 1923–1941* 64  (1-55713-185-6, $12.95)

TOM RAWORTH [England]
  *Eternal Sections* 23  (1-55713-129-5, $9.95)

JEROME ROTHENBERG [USA]
  *Gematria* 45  (1-55713-097-3, $11.95)

SEVERO SARDUY [Cuba]
*From Cuba with a Song* 52 (1-55713-158-9, $10.95)

LESLIE SCALAPINO [USA]
*Defoe* 46 (1-55713-163-5, $14.95)

ARTHUR SCHNITZLER [Austria]
*Dream Story* 6 (1-55713-081-7, $11.95)
*Lieutenant Gustl* 37 (1-55713-176-7, $9.95)

GILBERT SORRENTINO [USA]
*The Orangery* 91 (1-55713-225-9, $10.95)

GERTRUDE STEIN [USA]
*How to Write* 83 (1-55713-204-6, $12.95)
*Mrs. Reynolds* 1 (1-55713-016-7, $13.95)
*Stanzas in Meditation* 44 (1-55713-169-4, $11.95)
*Tender Buttons* 8 (1-55713-093-0, $9.95)

GIUSEPPE STEINER [Italy]
*Drawn States of Mind* 63 (1-55713-171-6, $8.95)

ROBERT STEINER [USA]
*The Catastrophe* 134 (1-55713-232-1, $26.95 [cloth])

JOHN STEPPLING [USA]
*Sea of Cortez and Other Plays* 96 (1-55713-237-2, $14.95)

STIJN STREUVELS [Belgium/Flanders]
*The Flaxfield* 3 (1-55713-050-7, $11.95)

ITALO SVEVO [Italy]
*As a Man Grows Older* 25 (1-55713-128-7, $12.95)

JOHN TAGGART [USA]
*Loop* 150 (1-55713-012-4, $11.95)

SUSANA THÉNON [Argentina]
*distancias / distances* 40 (1-55713-153-8, $10.95)

JALAL TOUFIC [Lebanon]
*Over-Sensitivity* 119 (1-55713-270-4, $13.95)

CARL VAN VECHTEN [USA]
*Parties* 31 (1-55713-029-9, $13.95)

TARJEI VESAAS [Norway]
*The Ice Palace* 16 (1-55713-094-9, $11.95)

KEITH WALDROP [USA]
  *Light While There Is Light: An American History* 33
  (1-55713-136-8, $13.95)

WENDY WALKER [USA]
  *The Sea-Rabbit or, The Artist of Life* 57 (1-55713-001-9, $12.95)
  *The Secret Service* 20 (1-55713-084-1, $13.95)
  *Stories Out of Omarie* 58 (1-55713-172-4, $12.95)

BARRETT WATTEN [USA]
  *Frame (1971–1991)* 117 (1-55713-239-9, $13.95)

MAC WELLMAN [USA]
  *The Land Beyond the Forest: Dracula* AND *Swoop* 112
  (1-55713-228-3, $12.95)
  *Two Plays: A Murder of Crows* AND *The Hyacinth Macaw* 62
  (1-55713-197-X, $11.95)

JOHN WIENERS [USA]
  *707 Scott Street* 106 (1-55713-252-6, $12.95)

ÉMILE ZOLA [France]
  *The Belly of Paris* 70 (1-55713-066-3, $14.95)
                              *

Individuals order from:
Sun & Moon Press
6026 Wilshire Boulevard
Los Angeles, California 90036
213-857-1115

Libraries and Bookstores in the United States and Canada
should order from:
Consortium Book Sales & Distribution
1045 Westgate Drive, Suite 90
Saint Paul, Minnesota 55114-1065
800-283-3572
FAX 612-221-0124

Libraries and Bookstores in the United Kingdom and on the Continent
should order from:
Password Books Ltd.
23 New Mount Street
Manchester M4 4DE, ENGLAND
0161 953 4009
INTERNATIONAL +44 61 953-4009
0161 953 4090